TWINS

DR. NAGARAJ S. BHADRASHETTY

Made with ❤ on the Notion Press Platform
www.notionpress.com

To,
Veer Chethak Bhadrasetty.

Contents

" The author chronicles the evolving value systems of three societal epochs: Agricultural, Industrial, and Electronic, through the lives of the fictional Veerashetty family spanning three generations. "Twins" is the final instalment in this trilogy, preceded by "Maharudra" and "Chaos Don't Destroy."

"One must still have chaos in oneself to be able to give birth to a dancing star."
-Friedrich Nietzsche:

"When we are no longer able to change a situation, we are challenged to change ourselves."
- Viktor E. Frankl

....“ Once, when Dr Mahadev went to his village, he gathered the Dalits and tried to use the lake's water with police protection. The prominent Lingayats of the town met him and said, 'According to the law, you can use the lake's water. If we obstruct you, we'll be jailed. So we won't obstruct you. But know this, once you touch the lake's water, the entire village will stop using it. We've decided this in a meeting of all community leaders.'

Dr. Mahadev was shocked and stopped the movement. I asked him why he stopped the movement. He said, 'In our village of six thousand people, there are about six hundred Dalits. If I continued the movement and the Dalits touched the lake's water, the lake would have become just a Dalitlake. They said they would boycott the lake we touched. What can the law do here?”...

CHAPTER ONE

DITI

Diti sat on a bench at the bus stop in front of her college, the London School of Economics, puffing a cigarette. As a Diploma student in International Religious Beliefs, she often found herself, pondering deep philosophical questions amidst the bustling London streets. She lived alone in an apartment just a stone's throw away from the college. Despite owning a sleek Mercedes-Benz, she occasionally enjoyed the solitary walks to campus, savouring the crisp London air. Her black sunglasses, black skirt, and yellow t-shirt added to her distinctive appearance, complemented by her jet-black bob-cut hair. At twenty-one, her youthful vigour was undeniable.

As she exhaled a cloud of smoke, a young man approached her.

"Hi," he said, stopping in front of her. "Alone?"

"No, waiting for my cousin," she replied nonchalantly, her eyes briefly meeting his before returning to the busy street.

The young man, about twenty-three, wore black sunglasses and had a laptop bag, slung over his shoulder.

"Did the 43-number bus leave?" he inquired, glancing down the road.

"After I sat here, a couple of buses came and left, but I didn't notice their numbers," she said, her tone casual yet detached.

"I'm Varghese, John Varghese," the stranger introduced himself, extending his hand with a smile.

"I am Diti," she said, shaking his hand. There was a moment of connection, a shared understanding between two strangers in a vast city.

"May I sit here?" he asked, gesturing to the space beside her.

"Of course," she replied, sliding over to make room. As he settled, he continued,

"I am from India. You?"

"My parents moved here from India. I was born here. Which state in

India?" she asked, extinguishing her cigarette with a practised flick.

"Karnataka," he replied, his accent subtly tinged with the sounds of his homeland. "I came here for a job in a software company." he paused, and eyed her, " How do you find the city?"

"It's a blend of chaos and calm," Diti mused, her eyes scanning the skyline. "Every corner has a story, yet there's a sense of solitude which, I find comforting."

John nodded, absorbing her words.

"Do you miss India?"

"Sometimes," she admitted. "But London has its charm. What about you? Do you plan to stay here for life?"

" No, one day I will go back, I am from Bellary, its in the northern part of Karnataka" he said, a nostalgic expression on his face.

"Great, my parents are also from Karnataka," she said, a smile touching her lips.

As they spoke, a sleek car pulled up, and a young man stepped out, his presence commanding attention. He stood in front of Diti, his expression a mix of impatience and concern.

"Hi, why are you late?" she asked, standing up to greet him. Turning towards Varghese, she introduced,

"This is John Varghese, from India." Then, gesturing to the newcomer, she said, "This is Jayakeerthi, my cousin."

"Hello," Varghese said, extending his hand in a friendly gesture. However, Jayakeerthi ignored it, with his focus entirely on Diti.

"It's time, only five minutes left for the show. Come on," he said, grabbing her hand with a sense of urgency.

The sudden force of his pull caused Diti to stumble. In an instant, Varghese reacted, his hands reaching out to support her by holding her waist, preventing her from falling. The moment was charged with tension, as Jayakeerthi's eyes flared with anger.

"You rascal, how dare you?", Jayakeerthi shouted, his voice echoing with fury. He released Diti's hand and in a swift motion, punched Varghese in the face.

The impact sent Varghese reeling backward, his head striking the bench with a sickening thud.
Blood began to trickle from the wound, staining the pavement.

Diti gasped, her heart pounding in her chest.

"Jayakeerthi, stop!" she cried, rushing to Varghese's side. The scene had escalated far beyond what she had anticipated, and she felt a surge of guilt and helplessness.

Varghese winced, his hand instinctively reaching for the back of his head.

"I'm okay," he muttered before becoming unconscious. Jayakeerthi stood there, his chest heaving with anger.

"Let's go, Diti," he said, his voice softer but still firm. "We don't have time for this."

Diti hesitated, torn between her cousin's demand and the injured stranger who had tried to help her. She glanced at Varghese, her mind racing with conflicting emotions.

"Oh no, what have you done?" Diti exclaimed, bending towards Varghese, holding his hand, and helping him sit on the bench. Her heart raced as she moved his hair to see the bleeding point.

Jayakeerthi grabbed her hand, his grip firm and insistent.

"We are getting late for the show, let's go," he urged, pulling her towards the car.

Shaking off his hand, she rushed back to Varghese, her concern overriding any other thought. Following her, Jayakeerthi demanded, "Why do you care so much about this stranger?" His voice was tinged with frustration. As he reached out to touch her, she pushed him back, her eyes blazing with determination.

Suddenly, a police jeep screeched to a halt nearby, and two sturdy police officers got out, their expressions stern.

"What's happening here?" one of them barked, pulling a pistol from his waist and aiming it at them. Jayakeerthi and Diti raised their hands, standing still, their faces a mix of shock and fear.

The officer covered them while the other advanced with a torch, illuminating Varghese lying there, bleeding.

"Oh God! this is an assault case. Call 999 and detain them," he said, his voice authoritative. The gravity of the situation sank in as the police called for an ambulance.

Within moments, the officers took Jayakeerthi and Diti into their custody with handcuffs, their movements swift and practised. The cold metal of the handcuffs bit into their wrists, a stark reminder of the seriousness of the situation. Diti's mind raced, trying to process the rapid turn of events. She glanced at Varghese, who was now being attended to by the paramedics, his face pale.

As they were led to the police jeep, Diti's thoughts were a whirlwind of confusion and regret. She had only wanted to help, but now she found herself entangled in a situation far beyond her control. Jayakeerthi's anger simmered beside her, his eyes fixed on the ground.

The city lights blurred as they drove away, the weight of the evening's events pressing heavily on their shoulders. Diti couldn't help but wonder how a simple encounter at a bus stop had spiralled into such chaos.

"You are mistaken. This is not an assault. We don't even know who he is. I came to pick up my cousin when he suddenly fell and hit his head on the bench. We were just going to help him when you arrived," Jayakeerthi argued, his voice steady but desperate.

"Whatever you have to say, say it at the station. You can claim you were helping him. Maybe. But he is unconscious now. Once he regains consciousness and we will verify your story, we will release you if you are innocent. Until then, you will be in police custody." the police officer said, removing the handcuff from Jayakeerthi's wrist and leading him to the police jeep.

Jayakeerthi glanced at Diti, frustration and concern etched on his face.

"We will come by my car," he said, walking towards his vehicle. Meanwhile, an ambulance arrived, and two paramedics hurried to Varghese. They quickly assessed his condition, one of them making a call.

"Hello, this is Sergeant Kerry; is this Charing Cross Hospital?" Hearing a confirmation, he continued, "We have a head injury case. Male, around twenty-plus years old, unconscious. It's an emergency case, and we will be there in about ten minutes." Without waiting for a response, he turned off the phone and focused back on the patient.

Diti watched the scene unfold, her heart pounding. Sitting next to Jayakeerthi in the car, she trembled slightly.

As they drove towards the police station, the city lights flashed by, casting a surreal glow on the streets. Diti's mind raced, replaying the chaotic events in a loop. She glanced at Jayakeerthi, who was silently fuming, his knuckles white as he gripped the steering wheel.

At the same time, the ambulance sped towards Charing Cross Hospital, sirens blaring. The paramedics worked swiftly to stabilize Varghese, monitoring his vitals and administering first aid.

*** --- ***

At the police station, Diti and Jayakeerthi were led inside, the cold air and sterile lights adding to their sense of disorientation. The officers processed them, taking their statements and placing them in a holding area. The wait began, each minute stretching into eternity as they hoped for news of Varghese's condition.

"Your name?" the police officer at the station interrogated, his tone sharp and unwavering.

"Jayakeerthi," he replied, trying to maintain his composure despite the tension.

"Show your DL, identification documents, and all car records," the officer demanded. The policeman who had accompanied

Jayakeerthi placed the documents on the table. The officer began examining the documents thoroghly, his scrutiny thorough and meticulous.

*** --- ***

Meanwhile, in the hospital about a mile away from the police station, Varghese was admitted and laid in the emergency room, being examined by a doctor and an ambulance nurse. The air was thick with urgency as medical professionals moved swiftly around him.

"He has sustained a head injury and is unconscious. Admit him to the ICU. We need to do a head scan. Do we have any information about his relatives?", the duty surgeon inquired, his voice calm yet commanding.

"Sir, we have no information on his identity. He was found unconscious at the bus stop in front of LSE College. This appears to be a medico-legal case. We are investigating. From the documents found in his pocket, it seems he works for Waves and Waves Software Company," said the policeman, presenting the company ID card found in the young man's pocket to the doctor.

Upon inspecting the card, the doctor noted the details: John Varghese, Senior Manager at Waves and Waves Software Company, with a phone number for his residence.

The doctor instructed Head Nurse Anna Maria to call the number to get more information. When the call was made, a voice from the other end asked, "Who is speaking?"

"Hello, this is Head Nurse Anna Maria calling from Charing Cross Hospital. We have a patient named John Varghese admitted with a head injury. He is unconscious. This number was on his ID card, which is why I am calling..." she explained, only to be interrupted by the voice on the other end.

"Varghese is our boy. Did you say Charing Cross Hospital?" the voice asked, a hint of urgency creeping in.

"Yes, who are you, and how are you related to Varghese?"

Anna inquired, hoping to piece together more of the story.

"I am Father Christopher from the King of Kings Church. I will head to your hospital immediately. I will provide more details upon arrival," said the voice before hanging up.

Since the nurse had the speaker on, there was no need to repeat the conversation to the doctor.

"Alright, if he has left, he should be here shortly. Move the patient to perform a head CT scan and draw blood for a routine checkup," instructed the doctor. Nurse Anna noted down the instructions in the case sheet with precision.

*** ___ ***

Diti's parents, Dr. Bhushan and Dr. Bharati lived in Birmingham, a city about one hundred miles away from London. Upon hearing the news, they left their home and arrived at Charing Cross Police Station.

Even though Dr. Bharathi was around fifty years old, her golden complexion and beauty still shone through her healthy and happy demeanor. Her round face bore a natural dignity that could unnerve anyone for a moment. Dr. Bhushan, a sturdy and attractive man, was close to fifty-two. He was wearing a vest and a British jacket. His tie and belt matched the brown Oxford shoes he wore, and his face was calm without any traces of emotion. His hair was silver at the temples, and he wore glasses.

"Diti is our daughter, and Jayakeerthi is our relative," Dr. Bhushan informed the police officer.

"First, introduce yourselves. Who are you, where are you from, and what do you do?" asked the police officer.

Before Bhushan could speak, Dr. Bharati interjected, "I am Dr. Bharati, and this is my husband, Dr. Bhushan. I have been serving as a gynaecologist at Queen Elizabeth Hospital in Birmingham for the past twentyfive years. My husband, Dr. Bhushan, is a professor at Birmingham University. Diti is our daughter, and Jayakeerthi is my cousin." "Are you a medical doctor as well?" the police officer asked, turning to Bhushan.

"No, I am a professor at Birmingham University," Bhushan replied. "Please show your ID and passports," requested the police officer.

Anticipating this, Bharati had brought their passports. Dr. Bhushan and Dr. Bharati placed their identity cards and passports, along with documents from their institutions and home addresses, on the table. The police officer examined each document and crosschecked it with the identification records held by Diti and Jayakeerthi.

"Alright, your identities are now officially verified. Let me explain the details of the incident," the officer said, recounting the events to them and instructing a nearby female officer to bring Diti. As soon as Diti arrived, she embraced Bharati, exclaiming,

"Mommy..."

"Where is Keerthi?" Bharati asked.

Following the officer's instructions, Jayakeerthi was also brought in.

"Look, sir, whether this was an accident, or an assault is yet to be determined. The injured person in the hospital is named John Varghese, around twenty-five years old. He is still in a coma. Only after he regains consciousness will we know the full truth. Until then, we must keep them in custody," the police officer explained.

"I am a law graduate. On what charges are you holding them in custody? Has anyone reported that they assaulted him?" Bhushan questioned.

The police officer stared at Bhushan for a moment before sharply responding " "Your card says you are an English professor. How can you say you are a law graduate?"

As Bhushan tried to respond angrily, Bharati stopped him, "Look, he is a law graduate, but he does not practice law. Is it necessary to be a practising lawyer to talk about the law? Now tell us, under which legal provisions are you holding them?"

Dr. Bhushan had earned his law degree from National Evening College in Bangalore.

The police officer stared at Bharati for a moment. The eyes behind her glasses seemed to pierce him sharply. The officer hesitated, composed himself, and shuffled in his chair, saying, "Look, Madam, we don't arrest anyone unnecessarily. Consider the circumstances. A person has sustained a head injury, is bleeding, and is in a coma. These two were present at the scene. Isn't it natural for anyone to suspect that this might be an assault case? You tell me," he said with a faint smile.

"Such suspicions arise only for a police officer like you," Bharati replied, smiling as well.

"Then what do you think happened?" the police officer challenged. Resting both hands on the table, her face on her left palm, and wagging her right index finger, Bharathi said, "Do you want to know what I think? Listen. I believe that while my daughter and cousin were at the bus stop, this person must have felt dizzy, fallen, hit his head on the bench, and collapsed. They must have gone to help him. Isn't it humane to help a stranger in such a situation? We should commend them, not punish them with blind legal suspicion, right?"

"As a doctor, you might think that way, and that's natural. But isn't it also natural for us police officers to have suspicions? If this turns out to be an assault case, and we release them based on your words, what if the person regains consciousness and claims he was assaulted? Wouldn't it be a dereliction of duty on our part for not arresting them?" he asked.

"Look, I am a professor at Birmingham University. My wife is a gynaecologist at Queen Elizabeth Hospital. Our daughter is a student at the London School of Economics. Jayakeerthi runs his own business in London. If you still have doubts, keep our passports. We will visit the station and the hospital daily to check on that person's condition until he regains consciousness. We will adhere to any lawful conditions you impose. But we don't see the need for them to remain in police custody. Permit us to take them home. If you refuse, we will have our lawyer come here," Bhushan declared, standing up and reaching for his mobile phone.

The sergeant said, "Please wait a minute, sir," and went inside. He returned a while later with a police inspector, who introduced himself and said, "Both of you must cooperate with us until he regains consciousness." "What do you mean by cooperate?" Dr. Bharati asked.

"First, bring their passports. We don't need yours. Next, you must visit the hospital and station daily to check his condition. Only after he regains consciousness and gives his statement will we proceed. There is no need for lawyers at this stage. We will not arrest them. Deposit their passports and you can take them home," said the officer, standing up and addressing the sergeant.

"Once their passports are brought, get a written assurance from them and release them," he added, heading to his chamber.

After he left, the sergeant, still seated, turned to Dr. Bhushan and said, "As the officer mentioned, bring their passports and you can take yours back." and gave them a printed form, and added, "Fill this out and return it." To fetch Diti and Jayakeerthi's passports, Bharati and Bhushan left the station.

*** --- ***

Meanwhile, Reverend Father Christopher arrived at the hospital, identified John Varghese, and said, "This is our boy. Provide him with the necessary treatments. I am his godfather. I will fill out the necessary forms.

After filling out the hospital forms, he went to the nearby police station. By then, Dr Bhushan and Dr Bharati had arrived with Diti and Jayakeerthi's passports. Inspector Robert Louis introduced them.

"Why did you ask for their passports? They were helping Varghese, weren't they?" asked Father Christopher, sitting down.

"That is not yet confirmed, Father. We will know for sure once he regains consciousness. Until then, it is natural and lawful for them to be under suspicion," said Louis.

"What if he regains consciousness and says they were helping him?" Father Christopher asked sharply. "Then we will return their passports, Father," said the sergeant.

"Let the passports stay with them. We don't need them now. He may regain consciousness in a couple of days. They can return the passports then," Bharati interjected.

"Please introduce yourselves once more," Father Christopher asked, turning to the couple.

"My name is Dr. Bhushan. I am a professor at Birmingham University. This is my wife, Dr. Bharati. She is a medical doctor, while I am a scholar. We live in Birmingham. Diti is our daughter, a student at LSE. She lives in London..." Bhushan was interrupted by Bharati, "Jayakeerthi is my nephew. He runs a Restaurant in London," she said.

"Thank you for introducing yourselves. I am Father Christopher Mascarenhas, a pastor at the King of Kings Church. John Varghese is our boy. He resides in the dormitory on our church premises," he said, turning to the inspector.

"These are respectable individuals in prominent positions. One is a doctor treating pain, and the other is a professor shaping future generations. Naturally, we would expect their children to be well mannered. If our boy regains consciousness and says they were helping him, what then?" he asked sternly.

The flustered inspector replied, "What do you suggest we do, Father?"

"To start with, return their passports," Father Christopher said. "How is that possible, Father? What if this is an assault case?" asked the officer.

"Even if it is an assault case, neither I nor our boy will file a complaint. Without a complaint, where is the case?" he said, "We are grateful to you for admitting our boy to the hospital on time.

The church and I are indebted to you. I and our members will take care of our boy. Do not impose any conditions on them; return all the documents you have taken from them," he ordered.

"Excuse me, Father, but if we do not interrogate suspected criminals, won't that be a dereliction of our duty?" the police officer asked, looking at Father Christopher's face.

Father Christopher smiled gently, "Do you think I am interfering with your duty?" he asked.

"No, Father. Until it is definitively clear that they are innocent, it is standard procedure to keep them under police surveillance, isn't it? If we release them completely from legal scrutiny, it will seem like we are encouraging crime, wouldn't it?" the officer argued.

"Look, there is no proof of their crime. Even if they were criminals, I have said we would not file a complaint. Without a complaint, where is the need for an investigation?"

"If we release suspected criminals without interrogation, how is it, Father?"

"Remember what Jesus said when he saw those who crucified him?

'Father, forgive them, for they do not know what they are doing.' That is Christian compassion. If we do not embody it in life, how can we call ourselves followers of Christ?"

"It makes sense for you to say that as a Father. But is it possible for me, working in the police force, to do the same?"

"Certainly, it is not natural for you; I understand. That is why churches exist—to guide you on God's path. Divine justice is greater than all justice. Let it be. It might be difficult for you to decide within your jurisdiction. I will speak to your commissioner. Take me to his chamber," Father Christopher demanded.

"One minute, Father. I will go and ask the commissioner myself, please," the sergeant said, standing up and going to the commissioner's chamber.

After a while, the commissioner himself arrived, took Father Christopher's hand, and kissed it, "Forgive us, Father. If any of our boys acted recklessly out of ignorance, I apologise on their behalf. We will return all their documents. Let them take their children home. There is no need for them to come here or to the hospital again," he said humbly, bowing his head. The police had briefed him on the case.

"Thank you, Commissioner D'Souza," said Father Christopher, turning to Bhushan and Bharati. "Please visit our church when you have time," he invited, shaking their hands.

*** ___ ***

After retrieving all the documents in police custody, Bhushan and Bharati assured they would visit the hospital daily until Varghese regained consciousness. They thanked Father Christopher and left. Diti and Jayakeerthi accompanied them to their home in Birmingham.

"Why were you at the bus stop and why did Keerthi come there?" Bharati asked her daughter?"

They were all seated on the sofa in their Birmingham home.

Diti who had not fully recovered from the agitation said, "Keerthi had called yesterday suggesting we go see a Rajinikanth movie at the Moonlit Multiplex. I told him to come near the bus stop in front of my college. I went there after my class to wait for him. While I was waiting, Varghese came and asked about the bus, so I was talking to him. Then Keerthi came and pushed him without any reason. I went to introduce him as he was also from Karnataka, but Keerthi didn't care and hurriedly pushed him. Why did he need to push him?"

"Why were you acting so familiar with him? What was the need to befriend him?" Keerthi retorted, "He asked about the bus he needed to take. What's wrong with me talking to him about that? After knowing he's from India, I got interested," "Hundreds of Indians come to my Restaurant. If I sit down and chat with them like you do, I'd have to close my Restaurant and move to Thanjavur. Grow up, Diti. If you had just said bye to him and sat in the car, this fuss wouldn't have happened. Why should I bother about his introduction? You're blaming me for your mistake?" Keerthi fumed.

Keerthi was six years older than Diti. He ran the "East-West Restaurant" in London. His ancestral property in Thanjavur was plentiful and he could have been an administrator and a politician like his grandfather, Dr Bharati's father, Varadaraja Iyengar, who was elected MLA six times but refused ministerial posts. However, Keerthi had no interest in this and started a Restaurant business in London.

He also had a desire to get closer to Diti and marry her under the guise of running his business. Even though Dr. Bharati didn't like her nephew's venture, she supported him, succumbing to his persistence. Keerthi's father, Bharati's brother Narasimha, also wasn't happy about his son staying in London.

"Alright then, I am a fool? You're so smart, tell me how you'll handle this," Diti challenged him, crossing her legs.

"What's there to handle? It's already resolved. Our passports have been returned, and we don't need to go to the police station or the hospital. What else is there to do?"

"That's fine for now, thanks to Father Christopher's kindness. But what if Varghese regains consciousness tomorrow and tells the police that he fell and hit his head because you punched him?

What will you do then?" Bhushan, who had been silent until then, questioned.

"We'll handle it if that happens, Uncle. I don't think he will say that. He knows it happened accidentally. So, it won't be a police case. For an act to be a crime, there must be intent. What's the intent here, Uncle? Even if anything happens, we might have to spend some money. That's it. I hurried Diti saying we were getting late for the show. If she had just come with me, this wouldn't have happened." Keerthi said, looking at Diti's face.

"I'm not a little girl. Why did you pull my hand? It's my choice who, and what I talk to. Even Mom and Dad don't interfere with my freedom. Who are you to question me? Don't poke your nose in my personal affairs again. Don't you come near my college or apartment. We can meet only at this home. Keep that in mind," Diti snapped back, got up, and briskly walked away toward her room.

*** ___ ***

The next day, around eleven o'clock, Diti went to the hospital to see Varghese. He was still unconscious. Father Christopher was there.

"Good morning, Father. Mom told me that you helped us get our passports back. Thank you very much," she said, introducing herself.

"Dear, unexpected events happen in life to test our beliefs and values. Don't worry. He is still unconscious. The doctors say all the investigation reports are normal. Although he has a slight head injury, there is no internal bleeding. It's his luck. The brain swelling has decreased, and he could regain consciousness at any moment, the doctor says. There is no need to panic," he said soothingly.

Diti looked at Varghese. He hadn't opened his eyes, and his head was bandaged. A small amount of mannitol drip was slowly entering his bloodstream through an IV.

Father Christopher inquired about her college and studies and added, "You should attend to your classes. There's no need to come here daily. I will call you as soon as he regains consciousness." Thanking him and giving her mobile number, Diti left. That evening, Bhushan and Bharati also visited the hospital, but Jayakeerthi neither went to the hospital nor the police station. Bharati and Bhushan were constantly worried about what Varghese might say when he regained consciousness.

*** --- ***

On the third day, around ten in the morning, Varghese regained consciousness. Diti, who had come to see him, was in his hospital ward. The doctor examined him thoroughly and ordered another set of investigations, and the police were informed.

"May I speak with him?" Diti asked the doctor. "Yes, but avoid complex and probing questions," Diti approached Varghese. "Hello,"

"Hello."

"Do you remember me?" she asked with a smile.

"Sorry, I don't," he replied.

"Please, the police are here. Let them speak." the doctor said, Diti stepped back from the bed. The sergeant recognised her and said, "Hi," Diti responded,

"Hi."

"Didn't your cousin come?"

"No, should I call him?"

"No need, let's see," he said, approaching Varghese, who was sitting up with his legs stretched out "Hi," he greeted him.

Varghese raised his hand, "Hi."
The doctor introduced the sergeant, "This is the sergeant from Charing Cross Police Station. They brought you to the hospital."

He signalled Diti to come closer and asked Varghese, "Do you recognise her?" Diti stepped closer, and Varghese looked at her for a moment before saying, "Oh, were you the one I was talking to at the bus stop that day? Sorry, I forgot your name," he said with a faint smile.

"My name is Diti," she said, extending her hand.

"Varghese, John Varghese," he said, shaking her hand. "Wasn't there someone else with you that day?" he asked.

"That's what I'm here to ask. We suspect that her cousin attacked you, causing you to fall and injure yourself. What do you say?" Before Diti could answer, the sergeant interrupted.

John leaned back against the pillow and said, "What are you saying? They came to help me."

"Then how did you fall and hit your head on the bench?" he asked. Another officer who was standing beside him was writing down the conversation in a notebook.

"That day, I had breakfast in the morning but hadn't eaten till evening. She was beside me. I had asked her about the city bus to go to my church. While we were talking, a young man came looking for her. When she was introducing him, I suddenly stood up and shook his hand. I felt dizzy, everything went dark, and I fell. I don't remember anything after that."

"Did you know Diti and her cousin Jayakeerthi before?"

"No, I saw them for the first time at the bus stop. I just learned now that the person with her was her cousin. I had never seen them before," said Varghese, turning to Diti. "When I felt dizzy and fell, you and your cousin must have helped and brought me to the hospital. Thank you. Where is your cousin?"

"He runs a Restaurant here. I'll bring him to meet you another time," she said.

"How long does he need to stay here?" turning to the doctor, she asked.

"He is fully conscious and has no other issues. He can be discharged tomorrow if he wants. He will need to come back in a week to have the stitches removed," the doctor replied.

Meanwhile, the police sergeant asked Varghese, "Why were you at the bus stop that day?"

"Look, sir, on that day I went to LSE College by city bus to get information about their courses. While waiting for the bus to return, I met her at the bus stop, that's all. I don't understand why you are making such a big deal out of this," "Now, it seems like a small matter to you, and it's easy to say nothing happened. But for us police, this is a serious issue. Here we have two young men and a young woman; it's natural for us to suspect that this could be a case of assault stemming from a love affair. If we don't investigate, the newspapers and TV channels will tarnish the police's reputation, you know?"

At that moment, Father Christopher arrived. The sergeant greeted him. Father Christopher went to Varghese, gently patting his head, and asked, "How are you?" "I'm fine, Father," Varghese replied, sitting up straight.

The doctor greeted Father Christopher, "He has regained consciousness and everything is normal. He can be discharged tomorrow." Father Christopher thanked the doctor and turned to the police sergeant, asking, "Is your investigation over and complete?"

"Yes, Father. He says he fainted and fell on his own. Since there are no complaints or disputes, our duty here is done. He is fortunate to be unharmed and in good health, which is a relief for us,"

"Thanks to you, our boy received timely hospital admission and proper treatment. This is a commendable act in the eyes of God. Kudos to your sense of duty," Father Christopher said, shaking the sergeant's hand again.

"It is our duty, Father," the sergeant replied. Turning to Varghese, he added, "Before you get discharged, you come to the Police station and write a statement."

"He will come and do as you requested. God bless you." Before Varghese could respond, Father Christopher said,

*** ___ ***

"Do you know who this is?" Diti asked Keerthi, pointing towards Varghese. It had been a month since the incident, and they were having breakfast at Keerthi's Restaurant on a Saturday morning. Despite Diti's insistence, Keerthi had never visited Varghese in the hospital.

"No, I don't know. He must be a student from your college," Keerthi replied nonchalantly, standing up and extending his hand towards Varghese.

"Hello, nice to meet you."

"Me too," Varghese replied, shaking his hand firmly.

"This is Varghese, who fell at the bus stop and got admitted to the hospital with a head injury. He's my new friend," Diti announced, her voice steady and clear, yet carrying an underlying challenge.

Keerthi's expression shifted from casual curiosity to one of shock and confusion. "Your friend?" he echoed, struggling to process the revelation.

"Yes, Keerthi," Diti confirmed, her eyes locked onto his, "Varghese and I have gotten close since the incident. He's no stranger now. He's someone I care about." Varghese looked slightly uncomfortable but managed a polite smile.

Keerthi's face hardened, a mix of emotions battling within him. "I see," he said.

Diti, sensing the underlying tension, decided to steer the conversation to safer ground. "How's the restaurant doing, Keerthi? Busy as always?" Keerthi took a deep breath, forcing a smile.

"Yes, very busy. Business is good," he replied, though his tone lacked warmth. "Hey Diti, come here for a minute." As they were about to leave the Restaurant, Keerthi called out, His tone was unusually commanding, drawing Diti's attention immediately. She approached him, curiosity and slight annoyance mingling on her face.

"I'm going to Birmingham this evening. Make sure you come too," he said curtly. Diti stood there for a moment, taken aback by his abruptness. She glanced at Varghese, who had been observing the interaction from a distance, concern evident in his eyes. "Is everything alright?" Varghese asked as she returned to him.

"No problem, come." As they left the Restaurant, Diti's mind was filled with questions. She couldn't shake the feeling that something was off, yet she didn't want to jump to conclusions.

*** ___ ***

Back in her apartment, Diti had asked him, "Don't you remember what happened that evening?"

"I remember talking to you and you introducing your cousin, but nothing after that."

He didn't want to make a fuss and hurt the beautiful girl, so he told the police sergeant that he had fallen accidentally. He had decided it was an accidental incident and didn't want to blame anyone. Diti was attracted to his kind nature and accepted him as a friend. They started meeting on weekends, and Varghese liked her innocent and straightforward demeanour. They became closer, talking on the phone, meeting up, and spending time together happily. However, Keerthi had no idea of this until Diti introduced him to Varghese at the Restaurant. Despite coming from a respectable background, Keerthi lacked interest in studies. He barely managed to complete his B.A., and when he did, his father, Narasimha, remarked, "I didn't have to struggle this much to get my B.Sc.," laughing in front of his father, Varadaraja.

At that time, Varadaraja responded, "Winning over Saraswati (the goddess of Knowledge) is not as easy as winning over her sister Laxmi, (Goddess of Wealth) It's enough that he has completed his B.A. Did you expect him to study and get a job?"

"Even when I wanted to join M.Sc., you said the same things."

"Do you still remember that? You should also remember why I said it." Varadaraja retorted.
When Narasimha passed his B.Sc., he was adamant about marrying his classmate, Susan. Fearing that marrying a Christian girl would disrupt their family's lineage and tradition, and because Narasimha wanted to go to Madras to pursue her more than his M.Sc., Varadaraja refused to give his consent. He had investigated and found that Susan was joining the same college in Madras for her M.Sc.To prevent Narasimha from secretly marrying her, Varadaraja didn't permit it. Instead, he made Narasimha the principal secretary of the college administration and arranged his marriage with an Iyengar girl. Gradually, Narasimha forgot about Susan and got involved in college and family affairs. He hoped to make his son, Jayakeerthi, a skilled doctor like his sister, Bharati. However, Jayakeerthi, lacking interest in studies, passed his P.U.C. with thirdclass marks, dashing his father's hopes. Despite this, Narasimha was ready to pay a donation and make Jayakeerthi a doctor. Being a multimillionaire, paying a donation for an M.B.B.S. seat was not a big deal for him. But Keerthi refused and went to London with his aunt.

*** ___ ***

One Saturday evening around six, Jayakeerthi arrived at Bharati's house in Birmingham without notice. Despite not calling ahead, Bharati and Bhushan were home. Hearing the doorbell, she checked the peephole and saw Jayakeerthi standing there. She opened the door with a surprised smile.

"Come in! Why didn't you call first? Is something urgent?" she asked, leading him to the living room and turning off the TV.

"Why did you turn off the TV, Auntie? Nothing urgent. I just decided to visit. Where's Uncle?" Jayakeerthi asked as he joined her on the sofa, trying to sound casual.

"Uncle is in his room, probably reading something as usual," she said with a knowing smile, heading to the kitchen.

"Wait, I'll get some coffee for you." As she disappeared into the kitchen, Jayakeerthi leaned back on the sofa and turned the TV back on, flipping through the channels absent-mindedly. The familiar sounds of the news and commercials filled the room, but his mind was elsewhere. Moments later, Bhushan emerged from his room, a book in hand.

"Jayakeerthi! What a pleasant surprise," he greeted warmly, his eyes twinkling behind his glasses.

"Hello, Uncle. It's good to see you," Jayakeerthi replied, standing up to greet him.

"Sit down," Bhushan said, waving his hand. " How are you?"

"Fine uncle."

Bharati returned with a tray of steaming coffee cups. "Here you go," she said, handing a cup to each of them. She then sat down, her curiosity evident. "So, what brings you here so suddenly?"

Jayakeerthi took a sip of his coffee, savouring the warmth before answering. "I just wanted to discuss something important with you, and Uncle." Bharati and Bhushan exchanged glances, sensing the seriousness in his tone.

"Of course, Jayakeerthi. We're here to listen," Bhushan said, leaning forward slightly. Jayakeerthi hesitated for a moment, gathering his thoughts. "It's about Diti. There have been some complications recently, and I think we need to discuss this " Bharati's eyes widened slightly, her concern growing.

"What kind of complications?" Jayakeerthi took a deep breath, preparing to explain. The air in the room seemed to thicken with tension as they prepared to delve into the sensitive topic, knowing that the family dynamics were at stake.

"How's the Restaurant doing?" Bhushan changed the topic to ease the situation.

"Not bad, Uncle. It's profitable, but the staff turnover is frustrating. No one stays for more than two months. And the taxes here are exorbitant, eating into our profits," Jayakeerthi laughed, though there was a hint of exasperation in his voice.

"Maybe you should hire workers from India," Bharati suggested. "I've tried that. Local workers are disciplined, but our Indian workers lack cleanliness. I got several complaints from customers. It's hard to teach them hygiene," Jayakeerthi explained, shaking his head slightly.

"Why?" Bharati asked, curious.

"It's their upbringing, Auntie. If they maintained cleanliness in their daily lives, they'd do the same here. But they don't pay attention. Skilled workers demand higher wages. If they find a better-paying job, they leave. Unlike our workers, they don't leave debts or disappear without notice. That's why I stopped hiring Indian workers. Believing our people are ideal workers is an illusion," he concluded, his tone a mix of frustration and resignation.

Bharati and Bhushan listened quietly, absorbing his words. The challenges he faced were not uncommon in the business world, but it was clear they weighed heavily on him.

"Hasn't Diti arrived yet?" Bhushan asked, setting down his coffee cup, his brow furrowed with concern. "She called to say she'd arrive by eight," Bharati said, and turned to Jayakeerti, "Have you seen her?"

"Yes, she came to my Restaurant this morning," Jayakeerthi replied, his expression shifting to one of suspicion. "She was with that guy and I am here to discuss her."

"What guy?" Bharati asked.

"The same Christian guy involved in the police case against us. She came for breakfast with him at my Restaurant," he said, his tone hardening.

"What are you saying? He didn't file any complaint. He even told the police it was his fault," Bhushan objected, his voice calm but firm.

"But, it's true, we had to go to the police station because of him," he retorted, his tone dissatisfied and defensive.

Bhushan exchanged a concerned look with Bharati.

"Keerthi, you should understand that Varghese took responsibility for the accident. It was an unfortunate event, but it was not his fault," Bharati said gently, trying to diffuse the tension.

Keerthi shook his head, frustration evident on his face. "I am afraid, you don't understand the situation. I don't trust him. He's getting too close to Diti."

"Don't judge, trust her," Bhushan advised. "She's an adult and capable of making her own decisions."

"I just don't want her to get hurt uncle," Keerthi murmured, looking away.

"We all want to protect her, but we must also give her the freedom to live her life," Bhushan added, his voice soothing but firm.

"Look, Keerthi, If you had behaved more calmly that day, this would have happened. Why blame him unnecessarily?" Bharati asked, her tone both firm and compassionate.

"What do you mean, Auntie?" he asked, clearly taken aback.

"Diti explained the incident to me. According to her, how is he at fault, tell me?" Bharati asked seriously, her eyes locking onto Keerthi's.

"Let's not dwell on that now. It's over," Bhushan interjected, sensing the discussion was getting heated and wanting to steer it away from conflict.

"Maybe for you and me, it's over. But for Diti, this might be the beginning of a new chapter for her," Jayakeerthi said sarcastically, crossing his arms. Bhushan and Bharati exchanged glances, their concern deepening. "What do you mean?" they asked in unison, their voices filled with curiosity and a hint of worry. "It seems they've been in touch since that day and moving closely," Keerthi explained, his tone laced with disapproval.

"Even if they are, what's the problem?" Bharati asked, her voice calm but probing.

"It might not be a problem for you, but it is for me," Jayakeerthi said, standing up abruptly.

"Why don't you sit down and explain why it's a problem for you? I don't understand," Bhushan urged, his voice steady "I don't get it either. Please explain.". Bharati added, "Diti will be here soon. I'll explain then. For now, I'm going to rest upstairs," Jayakeerthi said, heading towards the guest room on the first floor.

"Diti isn't coming alone, so whatever you need to say, say it now," Bhushan insisted, his voice taking on a firmer tone.

Jayakeerthi turned back, curiosity and frustration in his eyes. "Who else is coming with her?"

"I've invited her friend for dinner as well," Bharati replied, her tone gentle but resolute.

"Which friend, Auntie?" Jayakeerthi asked, turning to Bharati.

"She's coming with John Varghese. Since you're already here, let's all sit together and have dinner." Bhushan added, Hearing this, Jayakeerthi's face darkened.

"Sorry, I'll come another time," he said, abruptly grabbing his overcoat from the stand and heading towards the door. His footsteps echoed with a sense of urgency and frustration. Bhushan started to follow him, concern etched on his face, but Bharati gently stopped him, signaling him to stay quiet. She understood that pushing Keerthi right now might only escalate the situation further. They listened silently as the door closed behind him and his car engine roared to life, the sound fading into the distance. With a heavy sigh, they returned to the living room and sat on the sofa, the weight of the talks pressing down on them.

"Why is he being so difficult?" Bhushan murmured, rubbing his temples in frustration.

"He's just worried about Diti. But he's handling it the wrong way," Bharati replied, her voice filled with empathy and concern.

"We need to give him some time to cool down. Maybe then we can talk to him and help him see things differently," Bhushan suggested.

"Yes, let's hope so. But for now, we should focus on Diti " Bharati said, placing a comforting hand on Bhushan's arm. The room fell into a contemplative silence, the ticking of the clock the only sound breaking the stillness. They both knew that the coming days would require patience, understanding, and open communication to mend the familial rift and navigate the complexities of their relationships.

*** ___ ***

Back at the Restaurant, Jayakeerthi went to his private room, took four sleeping pills from under the bed, drank some water, and collapsed onto the bed without changing his clothes. The weight of the day's events pressed heavily on him, and he sought solace in the numbing embrace of sleep.

Keerthi had been taking one sleeping pill every night before bed. Gradually, he needed two pills to fall asleep. Sometimes, his friend Harris would stay over, and they would inject drugs into each other before sleeping. The ritual had become a dark secret between them, a way to escape the pressures of their lives.

Although no one else knew, Ramalingam, who cleaned the room daily, was aware. Ramalingam, around sixty years old, had worked in Keerthi's father's estate in Thanjavur. Varadaraja, Keerthi's grandfather trusted Ramalingam and sent him to look after Keerthi. Occasionally, Ramalingam would accompany Keerthi to Dr.

Birmingham's house but never mentioned Keerthi's drug use to anyone. He kept a close watch on Keerthi, believing it was his duty to protect the family's reputation. Varadaraja would occasionally call Ramalingam to inquire about Keerthi, but Ramalingam never mentioned the drug use, thinking it was just sleeping pills and believing it was harmless if it helped Keerthi sleep. He was unaware of the drug injections Harris and Keerthi used.

Harris, who had previously been the manager at Keerthi's Restaurant, left for a higher-paying job but remained friends with Keerthi. There was no ill will between them, and their bond was strengthened by their shared secret. Harris would often visit, and their nights would end in a haze of drugs and fleeting relief.

As Keerthi lay on his bed, the effects of the pills began to take hold.

His mind drifted into a foggy oblivion, the day's worries fading into the background. Ramalingam, ever vigilant, checked on him one last time before retiring for the night. He sighed, hoping that Keerthi would find a way to overcome his struggles.

The bedroom had become a sanctuary for Keerthi's hidden battles. The walls held secrets that only a few knew, and the shadows whispered of the challenges he faced. As the night deepened, the silence was broken only by the soft hum of the city outside, a reminder that life continued, even amid personal turmoil.

*** ___ ***

Half an hour after Jayakeerthi left, Diti and Varghese arrived at Bhushan's house. Bharati welcomed them and offered coffee. Diti turned on the TV while they sat on the sofa sipping coffee.

"Lower the volume; it interferes with conversation," she suggested. Diti turned off the TV.

"Are you from Ballari? Do you speak Kannada?" Bhushan asked Varghese in Kannada.

"Yes, Uncle. I studied in Kannada medium until my SSLC," Varghese replied in Kannada.

They continued conversing in Kannada. Although Bharati could not read or write Kannada, she understood the conversation. Diti, however, understood only a little Kannada but could guess the context. Bharati's native language was Tamil and Bhushan's was Kannada, so they usually spoke in English at home. Bharati went to the kitchen while Diti got engrossed in the TV. Bhushan and Varghese moved to a bench near a pond in the backyard.

"Looking at you, one might think you're French," Bhushan remarked with a smile.

"Why, Sir?" Varghese asked, laughing. "Your facial features and your complexion. It's so fair that one wouldn't immediately guess you're from India. Your accent reveals your Indian origin. Perhaps you get your features from your mother," Bhushan said, smiling.

"No, Sir. I got them from my father. He was very fair," Varghese replied.

"Is he still around?" Bhushan asked. "No, Sir. He passed away before I was born," Varghese said, fidgeting slightly.

"Sorry, I was just curious. Don't take it the wrong way," "No problem, Sir. It's a natural question," Are you also from Ballari, Sir?" Varghese asked.

"Who told you?"

"Diti mentioned it while we were talking," "Yes, but only from Ballari district. My hometown is Kotturu. Do you know it?"

"Yes, Sir. Before coming to London, my mother took me to Kotturu. She took me to a temple there for a ritual. We got off the bus, went to the temple, and then returned to Ballari by bus. That was the first and last time," Varghese recalled.

"Which temple was that?"

"I don't remember the name, but my mother said it was a famous temple in the area," Varghese said.

"Was it a church?"

"No, Sir. It was a Hindu temple."

"Then it must have been the Guru Basaveshwara or Kottureshwara Temple. It's a very famous temple. People of all castes and religions visit it. I was born and raised there. I studied there until high school. Hindus, Muslims, Jains, and Christians all visit the temple.

Its sanctity is such. No wonder your mother took you there." He paused and as an afterthought said, " One of my brothers lived in Ballari."

"Is he still in Ballari, Sir?"

"No, he passed away about twenty years ago," Bhushan said with a hint of sadness. "Was it due to an illness sir?"

"Nothing like that. He died in a railway accident," Bhushan said.

"Sorry to hear that, sir. What did he do in Ballari?" Varghese asked.

"He worked at a printing press there. Let's not dwell on it—it was a tragedy."

"My mother also worked at a printing press long before I was born. Perhaps they might have known each other. What was his name, sir?" Varghese asked.

"His name was Bhadrappa. Let's not revisit those unfortunate memories, It's getting dark; let's go inside." Bhushan said, standing up.

*** --- ***

Diti was busy with her postgraduate diploma studies, spending most of her time in front of her laptop. Varghese would visit her apartment on Saturdays or Sundays. During his visits, they would discuss her thesis topics, and Varghese would help her find the necessary information from the internet. They often made coffee and chatted, usually going out only after finishing her work. Varghese found it hard to tolerate Diti's smoking but never said anything to her. Once, when Diti offered him a cigarette, he declined, saying he didn't have the habit. When she asked if he drank beer, he laughed and said he did occasionally, in good company and mood.

"Why do you smoke so much?" Varghese asked Diti, his voice tinged with concern.

They were sitting in her apartment room, the soft glow of the lamp casting a warm light.

It was Saturday night around 8 PM, and Diti had called Varghese over because her laptop had hung. If she takes it to a computer shop, it would take two or three days to fix. She had a seminar on "Religious Beliefs and Rituals" at her college on Wednesday and needed to gather and compile information from the internet. Varghese came over and fixed her laptop. Just in case, he had also brought his laptop.

"It's just a habit. All the girls I hang out with, smoke and drink beer. Do you drink beer?" she asked. Varghese shook his head.

"I don't have the habit. Since coming to London, I've only had beer occasionally at office parties due to peer pressure. But I can't stand the smell of cigarettes. The smoke gives me a slight headache. Don't your parents object to your habits?"

"Why wouldn't they? Mom made a big fuss when she first found out. Dad just told me not to smoke too much. Without cigarettes, I can't concentrate on my studies. I only drink beer when I'm in good company or feeling down. Don't let it bother you. I'll put out this cigarette now. You search for the topic on the laptop," she said, stubbing out the cigarette in the ashtray.

"Which topic? Sorry, I forgot," Varghese asked, glancing at the laptop.

"The rituals, rules, and prohibitions in marriage ceremonies across different religions. Search on Google and Wikipedia. I'll be back soon," she said, taking the ashtray. When Diti returned, she brought two beer bottles from the fridge, placed one in front of Varghese, and started drinking the other. Varghese diligently searched for information on the laptop, printing out the relevant details from Google and Wikipedia. He handed the pages to Diti, who glanced through them while sipping her beer.

"It looks like you've dug up everything on the topic. How many pages are there?" She counted, "Twenty pages. I don't need this much for my thesis."

"This is a headache. I'll do it later. This is enough for now. Why don't you want beer?"

"It's 9 PM now. If I drink beer and Father finds out, he might be upset. I'll leave now. If you need anything else, I'll leave my laptop here," Varghese said, standing up.

"Would Father object to you drinking beer? I can't believe that" "It's a self-imposed restriction," Varghese smiled.

"How come?"

"When I first came here, on an evening, I was having dinner with Father and he offered me beer. He had some in his glass too. I refused, saying I didn't have the habit. Back in Ballari, I never drank beer. After coming here, I started having it at office parties to avoid being teased by colleagues. But I never drink when I am alone, only in good company, and then just one bottle—social drinking. If I drink beer now and Father finds out, he might think I drink secretly and be disappointed. I could have it someday in his presence, but for now, tea or coffee makes me happier than beer. Maybe I'm still old-fashioned," he chuckled.

Diti moved closer, took his laptop bag, "Stay here tonight. If you don't want beer, I'll make you some coffee. You can help me finish my thesis tonight. Has Father forbidden that too?" she added, placing the bag on the dining table.

"Not at all. If I call and tell him, he'd say 'alright.' It wouldn't be the first time. Sometimes I stay overnight at colleagues' places to discuss company projects, and he knows that. But is it necessary for me to stay here?"

"If you stay, I can complete my thesis tonight. Plus, I'm curious to hear more about your hometown and family, if you don't mind,"

"Alright, I'll call Father," Varghese said, picking up his phone.

*** ___ ***

Jayakeerthi's peace of mind was disturbed and was constantly simmering inside. He believed it was his right to marry his cousin Diti, and he couldn't stand her being so close to Varghese. In the social environment of India, he could have brought her under his influence through his father and grandfather. But in the English society of London, it was not easy. If things continued like this, Diti might slip away from him. He was tormented, wondering how to curb her free-spirited behaviour, which he believed was unbecoming of his future wife.

One Saturday night, while smoking marijuana with his friend Harris in his private room, he decided to share his problem. The room was filled with a hazy cloud, the smell of marijuana lingering in the air.

"Do you love her?" Harris asked, exhaling a puff of smoke, his eyes narrowing as he scrutinized Jayakeerthi's face.

" If I didn't love her, why would I bring up her matter with you? Do you have any advice or not?" Jayakeerthi replied, his frustration mounting as he took a deep drag, the smoke filling his lungs.

"It's not that, buddy. First, you need to be clear. Liking a girl is different from being fond of her, loving her, and wanting to marry her. That's why I asked," Harris explained, his tone calm but firm.

The distinction was crucial, but Jayakeerthi didn't understand. "What do you mean?" Jayakeerthi asked, his confusion evident.

"Who is Diti?" Harris asked again, probing further.

"Why are you asking like this? Diti is my cousin," Jayakeerthi replied, a hint of impatience creeping into his voice. "Can you tell me a bit about your family background?" Harris asked, leaning back and taking another drag.

"Why?" Jayakeerthi asked, suspicious of where this line of questioning was heading.

"I don't know much about it, and to give you proper advice, it would be good to know about your family," Harris explained, his tone thoughtful. Jayakeerthi sighed, realising that if he wanted genuine advice, he was to open up.

"Alright, I'll tell you. My family is quite influential back in India. My grandfather, Varadaraja Iyengar, was a respected politician and elected MLA six times. My father, Narasimha, manages our ancestral properties in Thanjavur. Despite their expectations, I chose to start a Restaurant business in London. I've always felt a deep connection to Diti. I believe she should marry me. But here in London, it's hard to impose those cultural expectations on her." Harris listened intently, nodding occasionally.

"I see. Your family's influence back home is strong, but here, it's different. You can't control her actions like you might be able to in India." Jayakeerthi nodded, the frustration evident in his eyes.

"Exactly. I feel like I'm losing her to Varghese. She's so independent, and I can't stand the thought of her being with someone else."

Harris took a deep breath, his expression serious. "If you truly love her, you need to respect her choices and independence. Trying to control her will only push her away. You need to have a conversation with her, express your feelings honestly, and win over her."

Jayakeerthi considered Harris's words, realizing the truth in them.

The path ahead was uncertain, but he knew he had to approach it with care and understanding.

"Diti is the daughter of Dr. Bharati and Dr. Bhushan. Bharati is my father's sister, so Diti is my cousin. Her father is a professor at Birmingham University, and her mother is a doctor at Queen Elizabeth Hospital," Jayakeerthi began, his voice steady as he recounted the details.

"Is Diti their only daughter?" Harris asked, his curiosity piqued.

"They have another daughter named Aditi. both are twins,"

"I see. Is Aditi also here in the UK?" Harris asked, leaning forward slightly.

"No, Aditi is in Bangalore,"

"Is she studying there?"

" Yes, she lives with my aunt and, is doing her medical course at a medical college there. Now she's pursuing her post-graduation," Jayakeerthi said, getting up and heading to the cupboard.

He returned with a family album and handed it to Harris.

"Look, here are Diti and Aditi with other relatives and friends."

Harris began flipping through the photo album, examining each page with an interest. They had stopped smoking the joint and were now engrossed in discussing the people in the album. Despite being under the influence, they remained cautious not to lose focus, understanding the seriousness of their conversation.

"That's Aditi, Diti's younger sister," Jayakeerthi pointed out, tapping on a photo of the two sisters standing side by side, smiling brightly at the camera.

"They look identical. Are they twins?" Harris asked, his eyes squinting slightly as he tried to distinguish between the two.

"Yes, they're the same age, born a few minutes apart. The first was named Diti, and the second is, Aditi,"

Harris viewed the photos even more closely, shaking his head in amazement. "I can't tell them apart. They look so alike, like the same person in both photos. Only your explanation tells me they're different."
    "That's because they're not just twins; they're identical twins," "I don't understand what that means," Harris said, looking up from the album, his brow furrowed in confusion.

"Those are details for another time. If you're curious, Google it later. Let's get back to the topic," Jayakeerthi said, waving a hand dismissively. He didn't want to diverge from the core issue at hand—his feelings for Diti and the complications that came with them.

Harris nodded, setting the album aside. "Alright, back to the matter at hand. You've got strong feelings for Diti, and it sounds like a complex situation, especially with your family dynamics. But you need to approach this with honesty and respect. Controlling her will only push her away."

Jayakeerthi sighed, rubbing his temples.

"I know you're right, but it's so hard. Seeing her with Varghese drives me crazy. I feel like I'm losing her."

"Then talk to her, man. Lay it all out. Be honest about your feelings and let her know where you stand."

The conversation continued late into the night, with Harris offering his support and guidance. For the first time in a long while, Jayakeerthi felt a glimmer of hope. He knew the road ahead would be challenging, but he was ready to confront his feelings and, hopefully, find a solution.

"I'm from Thanjavur, Tamil Nadu. My grandfather, Varadaraja Iyengar, is a prominent person, elected six times as an MLA. He has two children: his eldest son, Lakshmi Narasimha, who is my dad, and his second daughter, Bharati, Diti and Aditi's mother."

"Got it. You said Aditi lives in Bangalore with your aunt. How is that?"

"Aunt means cousin sister, not biological sister. My grandfather and my aunt Anuradha's father were cousins, understand? If you can't forget it. That is not relevant to what we are discussing now. "

Jayakeerti explained.

Harris nodded slowly, trying to piece together the intricate family tree.

"Okay, so Anuradha is Aditi's aunt. That makes sense."

"Exactly. Aditi lives with Aunt Anuradha in Bangalore Harris continued to flip through the photo album, absorbing the details of Jayakeerthi's family. "Your family seems close-knit. It's no wonder you feel so strongly about Diti," he remarked, looking up at Jayakeerthi. "Right," "I get it. So, Diti and Aditi are your aunts' children. You're in love with Diti and want to marry her. I see no problem here. Does Diti have a boyfriend?"

"That's the issue," Jayakeerthi said, holding his head in his hands, the weight of his frustration evident.

"What issue? Does she like someone?" Harris pressed, trying to get to the heart of the matter.

" Yes, she has a friend. Whether he's a boyfriend or just a friend isn't clear yet," Jayakeerthi admitted, his voice tinged with uncertainty.

"Who is he?" Harris asked, leaning in.

Jayakeerthi recounted the events from the bus stop incident to seeing John Varghese at Diti's apartment. Harris listened intently, his expression thoughtful. After contemplation, he spoke, "Show me who this Varghese is. I'll make sure he never comes between you and Diti." "What will you do?"

"I'll tell you later. I'm feeling sleepy now. Also, I need some money. I'll return it when I get my salary. Can you lend me some "How much?" Jayakeerthi inquired.

"A hundred pounds."

"I'll give it to you in the morning. It's late; let's sleep," Jayakeerthi said.

Harris nodded, and they settled into a more relaxed state, preparing to call it a night.

*** ___ ***

"Hello, my name is Diti. I am a final-year student of a diploma in World Religions and Beliefs at this college. Any Religion seeks to answer questions about human existence: who we are, our nature, how the universe began, or whether it has always existed. Is it eternal and infinite? Is there a divine force that created it, and if so, who created that force? What is the purpose of this creation, or is there no purpose at all? These and similar inquiries are what many religions around the world aim to address.

Several religions have emerged across different parts of the world, and today, I wish to discuss some of the major ones:
1. Hinduism
2. Buddhism
3. Islam
4. Christianity
5. Taoism
6. Judaism

Though there are many other religions, my presentation today will focus on these six. My friend John Varghese will assist with the presentation, focusing on images and other information on the screen. At the end, we will have a ten-minute Question and Answer session."

On Monday at 11 AM, Diti was presenting her thesis at the Academic Conference Hall. The program, initially scheduled for Thursday, had been postponed to the following Monday, as per the advice of her professor.

After her introduction, Diti provided an overview of the six religions, with images and data projected on the screen. About fifty students and four faculty professors attended the presentation. Among the external attendees were John Varghese, Jayakeerthi, and Antony Harris.

After her presentation, Diti's professor, Benjamin, took the mic and announced, "We now have a ten-minute question and answer session."

Harris stood up, "Which of these religions is the greatest?" Before Diti could answer, Professor Benjamin asked, "Please introduce yourself."

"My name is Antony Harris. I am the manager at Continental Restaurant."

Diti took the mic and replied, "It is natural for followers of each religion to believe theirs is the best. Therefore, comparing religions to determine which is superior is not relevant." "I didn't ask for your personal opinion. Academically, which religion do you consider the greatest?"

The room buzzed with murmurs. After a moment of silence, Diti turned to Harris and asked, "Among all the mothers in the world, which mother do you consider the greatest?" "My mother is the greatest of all mothers, to me," Harris replied.

"You've answered your question," Diti said with a smile.

There was a big applause with smiles. Another attendee took the mic and asked, "In Islam, cousins can marry. Is this allowed in Hinduism? Why do different religions have different marriage laws?"

"In Hinduism, cousins are considered siblings, so cousin marriages are not allowed and are against Hindu marriage laws," Diti explained. "But in Hinduism, children of siblings can marry. Since cousins share the same blood, why is it not prohibited? If one can marry their aunt's daughter, why not their uncle's daughter?"

"Scientifically and medically, cousin marriages are considered unhealthy due to genetic reasons. However, marriage laws vary across religions. In Hinduism, one can marry their aunt's children but not their uncle's. The question of 'why' is irrelevant here. These are long-standing practices. Each religion's beliefs are valid for its followers. These traditions have been followed for thousands of years and are not subject to logical scrutiny," Diti responded. "If Hindu cousins convert to Islam, can they marry?"

"If they convert to Christianity, the church may allow it. But as far as I know, it is not permitted in Islam. This depends on the laws of each country. There is no uniform marriage law across all countries,"

"Are you a Hindu?"

"Yes, I was born a Hindu, but I respect the practices of all religions. What is right in one religion shouldn't be wrong in another, in my view," Diti replied.

"So, if the situation arises, would you marry your uncle's son?" "I will marry the person I love, regardless of religious approval or disapproval.

As another attendee prepared to ask a question, Professor Benjamin, who was presiding over the session, announced, "That concludes the question-and-answer session," and ended the program.

*** ___ ***

"Everyone, this is Antony Harris. He used to be the manager at our Restaurant. Now, he's the manager at Continental Restaurant," Jayakeerthi introduced Harris to those around the table. After the seminar, as planned, they gathered for lunch at Jayakeerthi's Restaurant in a special room.

Along with Diti and Varghese, Dr. Bharati and Dr Bhushan were also present, having taken the day off to attend their daughter's seminar. The six of them were seated around the table, enjoying a South Indian special menu arranged by Jayakeerthi.

"You presented the different religions very effectively, without any bias. The origin, beliefs, and practices of the religions were beautifully illustrated with images and data, making it easy and impactful. Beautiful presentation, congratulations," Harris complimented. "Half the credit goes to John for his support," Diti responded.

"Who is John?" Harris asked. "Varghese, John Varghese," Diti clarified, pointing to him. Her casual use of his first name made Keerthi uncomfortable, a detail Harris noticed.

"Congratulations to you too," Harris said, turning to Varghese.

"I didn't do much. I was impressed with how you addressed the audience's questions. I do appreciate your view, love shouldn't be confined by religious boundaries," Varghese said.

"But I oppose converting to another religion just for marriage," Bharati shared her opinion.

"Why? What's wrong with that?" Bhushan asked.

"It's a matter of belief. Religion isn't just about marriage. It's deep and complex. It simplifies our lives, fosters harmony, and acts as a protective shield. Straying from it can lead to turmoil. That's my belief," Bharati explained.

"I don't see any danger in it. If it's risky, so what? No risk, no progress," Diti laughed.

"I agree with Auntie. Why take unnecessary risks?" Jayakeerthi added.

"Ultimately, it's about individual freedom. It's not right to set rigid rules on how one should live. Everyone has the right to shape their life as they see fit, as long as it doesn't harm others. Isn't that what you've done?" Bhushan smiled.

Bharati had married Bhushan against her parents' wishes, rejecting the groom they had chosen for her.
After finishing their meal, they thanked and bid farewell to Jayakeerthi. Bhushan and Bharati left for Birmingham in their car, while Diti drove off with Varghese.

Only Keerthi and Harris remained.

"How do you feel about it?" Keerthi asked Harris.

"About what?" Harris asked, looking intently at Keerthi.

"I'm talking about John Varghese,"

" Tell me, in which church does he live at?" Harris inquired. "King of Kings Church," "In Catford?"

"Maybe, I don't know."

"Got it. I'll go to that church for Sunday prayers. I'll inquire about him there "What are you thinking about?" Keerthi asked.

"I don't know what to do," Harris replied. "I'll start observing him at the church from next Sunday. I'll get to know the people there and gather information about him. Let's first collect more details about him and then plan our next steps. I'll call you another day to discuss this in detail." Harris took the money from Keerthi and left.

One Saturday, Diti and Varghese went to Oxford. Coincidentally, Harris was also there with his friends, and he greeted them. The next day, Harris visited Warwick Castle near Birmingham and noticed Diti and John Varghese again, observing them from a distance.

That night, while smoking marijuana, Harris shared, "I saw Diti and Varghese together."

"Where and when?" Jayakeerthi asked.

"We went to Oxford and Hardwick Castle over the weekend. We saw them at both places,"

Jayakeerthi took a drag and exhaled, looking at the ceiling. "In a way, it's my fault," he said, feeling remorse. "How so?"

"That day at the bus stop, if I had greeted him calmly instead of rushing, things might not have come to this," Jayakeerthi said regretfully.

Harris paused before responding, "If they are friends, so what? Just because they are friendly, why are you overthinking? If you want to marry Diti, you should talk to her and win her over."

"What do you mean by 'gently'? She's my cousin. I plan to talk to her parents and express my wish. I'm just waiting for the right time."

"When do her exams end?"

"I'll find out the next time I visit her house," "Alright, first propose to her, and then we'll see what happens," Harris suggested.

"What do you plan to do next?" Jayakeerthi asked Diti.

It was a Sunday morning, and he had visited Diti's house. Bharati, Bhushan, and the two of them sat around the dining table, sipping coffee after breakfast. Diti completed her exams in June and passed with distinction. "I have no concrete plans yet. I might go to Bangalore and spend some time with Aditi. We'll see," Diti replied, her tone casual yet thoughtful.

"I've been thinking of going to Thanjavur, maybe starting a business there. Life in London is getting boring. What do you think, Auntie?" Jayakeerthi asked, looking at Bharati.

"How long has it been since you started the restaurant?" Bharati inquired.

"It's been four years now,"

"The Restaurant is running profitably, right?"

"Yes, there's no problem with that. But life here feels empty and boring," Jayakeerthi replied, his voice reflecting a deeper dissatisfaction.

"Are you saying this like that, or are you serious?" Diti asked, laughing lightly, trying to gauge his seriousness.

"I'm seriously considering it, Diti. That's why I came here today to discuss it with all of you,"

"What do you plan to do with the Restaurant? Will you manage it or lease it out?" Bhushan asked, his tone pragmatic.

"I haven't decided yet, Uncle. But I've had enough of London's business and lonely life,"

"Look, Keerthi, you're the only son of your parents. Your sister Lakshmi will get married sooner or later. What is she studying now? I've forgotten," Bharati said, her voice gentle but concerned.

"Lakshmi is in her final year of B.B.M. at our college," Jayakeerthi replied.

"Isn't she four years younger than you?" Bhushan asked, trying to recall the family details.

"No, Bhushan. She was born six months after Diti and Aditi. She must be twenty-one years old now." turning toward Jayakeerti, she asked, "How old are you, Keerthi?"

Diti, uninterested in the conversation, stood up and headed to her room. "Why are you leaving, Diti?" Jayakeerthi asked a slight edge to his voice.

"I am tired and need rest" she replied, climbing the stairs without looking back.

"What is this, Auntie? I'm seriously discussing my future here," Jayakeerthi said, in disappointment.

"Keerthi, everyone has their way of dealing with things. Maybe Diti needs some time to think about her future also," Bharati said gently, trying to calm him down. "You're discussing your future with us, not with her, right?" Bhushan said, smiling.

"She also has a part in this discussion, Uncle. That's why I mentioned it," Jayakeerthi explained.

"If you had said that earlier, she might have stayed," Bharati suggested.

"Let me call her," Bhushan said, standing up.

"No need, Uncle. I'll ask her opinion another time," Jayakeerthi said. Bharati and Bhushan exchanged a surprised glance.

"You have given Diti a lot of freedom, Auntie," Jayakeerthi said, looking at Bharati.

"What do you mean by that?"

"Recently, she was touring with that Christian guy,"

"Keerthi, it's not proper to talk like that," Bhushan reprimanded.

"What do you mean, Uncle?"

"He's not just a Christian guy; he's Diti's friend, John Varghese. You know this, so don't speak carelessly."

Bharati nodded in agreement. "Sorry, Auntie, but I don't understand why she has to hang out with him,"

"Why shouldn't she, Keerthi? They're friends now, and he's a good guy. Plus, we're in London, not Thanjavur," Bhushan said, smiling.

"It seems like they're dating,"

"Alright, let's assume they're dating. So what?"

Bharati said, her tone mixed with dissatisfaction.

"I want to marry Diti, that's why," Bhushan looked at Bharati, who remained silent.

"I'll be straightforward. I plan to sell my Restaurant in London and move to Thanjavur. As you know, the property my grandfather and father has accumulated enough wealth to last generations. I can manage the estate, college, and fields, and enter politics as my grandfather. Despite being elected MLA seven times, the Congress party never made him a minister."

"That's not true," Bharati interjected. "Twice, the party offered him a ministerial position. I know this well. But he declined, saying, 'I don't want the hassles of being a minister. I'll stay in Thanjavur. I don't want the chaos of living in Madras and its politics.' He didn't want to contest the last two elections but did so under party pressure. So don't say the Congress didn't make him a minister."

"Really? I didn't know that. Anyway, the point is, that I plan to sell the Restaurant and move to Thanjavur and I want to marry Diti and take her with me. What are your thoughts on this?" Jayakeerthi asked directly, which Bhushan didn't appreciate.

"Have you discussed this with your parents and grandfather?" Before Bharati could speak, Bhushan asked him.

"Not yet. I wanted to know your opinion before telling them."

"Look, Keerthi, I like the idea of you marrying Diti, but it's not just about our approval," Bharati said.

"Who else, then? Should I ask my grandfather?"

"What are you saying? The one who needs to agree is Diti. Have you talked to her?" Bharati asked pointedly.

"I haven't brought it up with her yet. I wanted to know your opinions first.

So, do you approve of me marrying Diti?"

Bharati looked at Bhushan expectantly.

"Keerthi, I've known you since you were a boy. If Diti agrees and you marry her, I'd be happy. But first, find out her opinion. Then we can talk further," Bhushan said, looking at Bharati.

"I feel the same. First, get Diti's approval," Bharati occurred.

*** ___ ***

"Hello, Diti, it's Keerthi..." Jayakeerthi called Diti from his Restaurant one Friday morning,

"Hello, what's up?" Diti replied, sounding slightly distracted. "I need to discuss something personal with you. When can we meet?"

"I'm not available this Saturday or Sunday. Is it urgent?"

"Why? Where are you going?" Jayakeerthi probed.

"Why do you need to know? I'm not available, that's all. What's the matter?"

"It's not something I can discuss over the phone. Can we meet this evening?" Jayakeerthi suggested, hoping to convey the importance of the matter.

"Is it that urgent? Let's meet on Monday evening,"

"Alright, but not Monday evening. How about next Sunday?"

"Fine. If needed, I'll make time and come to your Restaurant"

Diti said, ending the call with a note of finality. Jayakeerthi suspected she had plans with Varghese that Saturday.

*** ___ ***

"Hello, Harry, where are you? I need to see you urgently,"

Jayakeerthi said, his voice carrying a bit of desperation.

Harris, sensing the urgency in his friend's voice, replied, "I'll come to your room tonight. We can talk then."

"She must have plans with Varghese. We need to do something to keep him away from Diti," Jayakeerthi said.

That night, Harris came over as promised. They sat in Jayakeerthi's private room, drinking beer and talking.

"What should we do?" Harris asked.

"I wouldn't be asking you if I knew. You need to come up with a plan," Jayakeerthi said, exhaling smoke from his cigarette filled with marijuana.

"First, you need to talk to Diti and understand her feelings. If she doesn't like you and we mess with Varghese, it could backfire. Think about it," Harris suggested.

"Diti is my cousin. There's no reason she wouldn't like me. You need to stop them from meeting frequently. Everything will fall into place after that," Jayakeerthi said, taking another puff.

"We need to find out if she's going out with him tomorrow and where they're going."

After a moment of silence, Harris said, "Alright, I'll find out and make sure he doesn't trouble Diti again. But..." he looked at Jayakeerthi.

"What is it?"

"It will cost some money," Jayakeerthi stared at him.

"What's your plan? What do you intend to do?"

"It's better if you don't know,"

"How much will it cost?"

Harris thought for a moment.

"A thousand pounds."

Jayakeerthi thought and then said, "Fine, do whatever you need to, but make sure it doesn't turn into a police case. I'll give you the money in the morning."

He believed that if Varghese stayed away from Diti, convincing her through his grandfather to accept him would not be difficult.

*** ___ ***

One Saturday morning at nine, Diti and Varghese were driving from London to Oxford in Diti's car, with Diti at the wheel. Detective Paul Drake and his associate Robert, hired by Harris, were following them in their car. Paul was a tall, intelligent detective with a lean build, while Robert was a burly, slow-witted man who looked like a wrestler. Although Diti had visited the famous university town before, Varghese had not, so they decided to go there at his request. After driving for about fifty miles, they stopped at a roadside

Restaurant for breakfast, having skipped coffee earlier. Among other tourists, they sat down while Diti went to the counter to order breakfast. Paul and Robert, who had been tailing them, also parked their car and entered the Restaurant. Paul went to the counter to get coffee, keeping an eye on Varghese.

As Robert walked past Varghese, he deliberately tripped over Varghese's outstretched leg and fell. Getting up, he turned to Varghese, who was startled and stood up to help him. Seizing the moment, Robert punched Varghese hard in the jaw, whispering, "Keep away from Diti," before walking out. The blow knocked Varghese to the ground, causing alarm among the other patrons.

Diti rushed over, exclaiming, "Oh God, what happened?" She bent down to help Varghese, but he was unconscious from the strong punch. Someone called for an ambulance, while a Restaurant staff member called the police. Before the police arrived, Paul and Robert had already left the scene, driving back towards London. The Restaurant buzzed with concern and confusion as patrons tried to make sense of the sudden violence. Diti stayed by Varghese's side, her heart pounding with fear and anger.

The ambulance arrived quickly, and paramedics began to assess Varghese's condition. "He has a concussion," one of them said, checking his vital signs. "We need to get him to the hospital." Diti nodded, her mind racing. She couldn't believe what had just happened. As they loaded Varghese into the ambulance, she followed closely. At the hospital, Varghese was taken for further examination. Diti sat in the waiting area, her thoughts a whirlwind of worry and anger. She knew she had to find out who was behind the attack and why they had targeted Varghese.

As she waited, her phone buzzed with a message from Keerthi. "Hey, Diti. Just checking in. How's your day going?" Diti stared at the message, her emotions boiling over. She decided to call him, needing to vent her frustration. "Keerthi, something terrible happened. Varghese was attacked at a Restaurant. He's in the hospital now," she said, her voice trembling. "What? Who did this?" Keerthi asked, his voice filled with genuine concern. "I don't know, but I intend to find out," Diti replied, her resolve hardening.

*** ___ ***

"This looks like an assault case, so let's file it as an MLC (Medicolegal Case)," said the duty doctor who examined John Varghese.

Varghese had been admitted to Oxford University Hospital, his face swollen and bruised. An X-ray revealed that three teeth on his left jaw were broken. By the time Varghese regained consciousness, the dental surgeons had already repaired the broken teeth, stopped the bleeding, and administered a couple of injections. They advised that hospitalization was not necessary. "What happened?" the police sergeant asked Varghese, his tone calm but inquisitive.

"I was getting up from my seat to go to the bathroom when I tripped over the leg of a burly man who was passing by. As I fell, I hit my face on the edge of a table. It was an accidental incident caused by my haste. No one is to blame," Varghese said, his voice steady despite the pain.

Although the doctor who examined him, had his suspicions that the injury was caused by a punch on his face, he did not press further as Varghese claimed it was an accident. Thus, it did not turn into a police case. The police took a statement from him and left without filing any charges.

*** ___ ***

Diti, who had been anxiously waiting outside the examination room, rushed in as soon as she was allowed.

"Varghese, are you okay? What happened exactly?" she asked, her voice filled with concern. Varghese managed a weak smile and said,

"I'm fine, Diti. It's a bit of bad luck. I'll be alright," he reassured her, though the pain in his jaw made it difficult to speak.

"Are you sure it was an accident? It looked like that man deliberately tripped over your leg," Diti insisted, her eyes searching his for the truth.

"It's best not to make assumptions, Diti. Accidents happen," Varghese replied gently, trying to calm her down. He didn't want to escalate the situation further or draw more attention to the incident. As they left the hospital, Diti couldn't shake off the feeling that something was off. She vowed to keep a closer eye on their surroundings and to find out more about the mysterious attack. Varghese's reluctance to confront the issue only deepened her resolve.

*** ___ ***

Back in London, Harris and Jayakeerthi were unaware of the full extent of the damage caused by Robert's punch. They assumed it was a simple scare tactic, never imagining it would lead to such serious consequences. But the events of that day would set off a chain reaction, bringing hidden tensions to the surface and forcing everyone involved to confront the realities of their intertwined lives.

"Why did you lie to the police?" Diti asked as she applied an ice pack to Varghese's swollen jaw. They were in Diti's apartment in London after returning from the hospital.

"What did I lie about? That's what happened," Varghese replied, grimacing in pain.

"I saw the burly man punch you in the face while I was holding my coffee cup. Why didn't you tell the police?" Diti asked.

"Please, let's not make an issue out of this. What's done is done. Let's forget about it," Varghese held her hand and said, "Why is this happening? There must be a conspiracy behind this. Do you have any enemies?" she insisted.

"Maybe, but I don't know. But we shouldn't make a big deal out of this," Varghese pleaded.

"You said the same thing the last time you got hurt. If you keep quiet, the world will trample over you. Being overly good isn't always a virtue; sometimes it's cowardice. Do you recognise the man who hit you?"

"Firstly, goodness isn't cowardice; it's a virtue. We read that Gandhi never hit back at anyone. Jesus taught, 'If someone strikes you on the left cheek, turn to him the right also.' We don't need to impress others or be disturbed by their insults. If someone thinks it's cowardice, so be it. As long as you don't think I'm a coward, it's enough for me," Varghese said, smiling through his pain and added,

"I don't know who that guy was. I've never seen him before."

"Alright, let it go. All I want is Varghese's friendship. I don't need someone who is like Jesus Christ. People don't hit others for no reason. There must be a reason behind this, and I will find out what it is," Diti said determinedly.

"I don't want any of this. If I don't want it, why do you need to? Please, let's drop this matter," Varghese pleaded, holding Diti's hand.

Though his calm and patient words increased Diti's interest in him, she realised that his passivity could lead to more trouble in the coming days. Silently, she decided to find out what was happening and who was behind it.

"Alright, let it go. All I want is Varghese's friendship. I don't need someone who is like Jesus Christ. People don't hit others for no reason. There must be a reason behind this, and I will find out what it is," Diti said determinedly, her resolve hardening.

"I don't want any of this. If I don't want it, why do you need to? Please, let's drop this matter," Varghese pleaded, holding Diti's hand tighter. His calm and patient words increased Diti's interest in him, but she realised that his passivity could lead to more trouble in the coming future. Silently, she decided to find out what was happening and who was behind it. As she sat there, her mind whirring with thoughts and plans, she couldn't help but feel a deep sense of protectiveness towards Varghese. She would get to the bottom of this, no matter what it took.

*** ___ ***

The next morning around ten, Diti drove alone to the roadside Restaurant they had visited the previous day. Determined to uncover the truth, she met with the manager and explained her purpose. The manager, a middle-aged man with a stern expression, listened patiently. They showed her the CCTV footage from the previous day. Diti watched intently, her heart pounding as she witnessed the incident Robert tripped over Varghese's leg and delivered the punch. The footage included audio, and she repeatedly listened to the faint voice saying, "Keep away from Diti."

It struck her immediately that this was Keerthi's doing.

"Can I record this footage and audio on my pen drive?" Diti asked, her voice steady but urgent.

The manager shook his head. "No, I'm sorry. We can't allow that."

"This is an assault case; I need this evidence to file a police report. Please help me."

The manager sighed, his expression softening slightly. "Why should I get involved in a police case? I'll only show this to the police if they come and ask for it." he replied.

"Alright, the police will come. Please don't delete this until then," Diti requested, The manager nodded. "I understand. We won't delete it."

*** ___ ***

Diti thanked the manager and left the Restaurant, her mind racing, with thoughts of what to do next. She knew she needed to act quickly to ensure the evidence was secured and find out more about Keerthi's involvement which she strongly suspected.

As she drove back to London, her phone buzzed with a message from Varghese.

"How did it go? Any luck?"

"I saw the footage. It was an assault. I'll file a police report. Hang in there," she switched off before he could say anything. Back in her apartment, Diti sat down with a cup of coffee, her resolve hardening. She would not let this incident go unanswered.

Keerthi had crossed a line, and she intended to hold him accountable. She began to gather all the necessary information to present to the police.

*** ___ ***

"Hello, good morning," Diti and Varghese greeted Jayakeerthi together. It was a Saturday morning, a week after the incident, and they had come to Jayakeerthi's Restaurant for breakfast. Jayakeerthi, who was sitting at the cash counter, stood up in surprise and greeted them back, "Hello. How are you?"

"Saturday is your special chow chow bath day, right? That's why we're here. Can we taste it?" Diti asked with a smile, "I wanted to have some kesari bath too, so I dragged him along," she continued, wrapping her arms around Varghese's waist.

"Come on, let's sit in my room and enjoy the kesari bath,"Jayakeerthi suggested, calling the manager to send enough hot khara bath and kesari bath for three to his room. The three of them walked to his private room on the first floor and sat around the small dining table.

Harris had met Jayakeerthi the day of the incident, claiming he had ensured Varghese would never bother Diti again, and had taken an extra hundred pounds from him. When Jayakeerthi asked for details, Harris said he would explain another time and left. Jayakeerthi, busy with the Restaurant rush, hadn't had the chance to question him further. He spent the week in anxious anticipation, afraid to call Diti. Despite multiple calls to Harris, he hadn't answered. Now, seeing Diti and Varghese together at his Restaurant, Jayakeerthi felt a mix of fear and irritation.

"Why does your jaw look a bit swollen?" Jayakeerthi asked Varghese.

"It's from a punching bag at the gym,"

"If you keep hitting it so hard, even the punch bag will hit you back," Diti added and turned to Jayakeerthi,

"What do you think, Keerthi?"

Her words stung Jayakeerthi. "True, we should always be careful with whatever we do to avoid such mishaps."

As they spoke, the Restaurant manager arrived with the breakfast boxes.

"Serve," Jayakeerthi instructed.

The manager placed the plates in front of them, served the food, and filled their glasses with water. "Coffee or tea, sir?" the manager asked.

Jayakeerthi looked at them. "Tea for me," Varghese said. "If you keep drinking tea, you'll get an ulcer. No tea," Diti interjected, "Apple juice for both of us,"

"Strong coffee for me," Jayakeerthi said.

"When did you last visit Ballari?" Jayakeerthi asked Varghese, trying to distract himself from his irritation.

Before Varghese could answer, Diti interrupted, "This khara bath is spicy. I can't finish it," and transferred her khara bath to Varghese's plate.

"What are you doing?" Varghese asked. "You said people in Ballari eat a lot of spicy food because of the heat. So, eat up," she said, emptying her plate into his.

"You and your ways, God bless you. You cancel tea saying it causes ulcers and now you're making me eat spicy food?" Varghese chuckled,

"Oh, sorry, I forgot. Here, let me take it back," she said, taking his plate and dumping the food into the bin. Though Varghese didn't realize it, Jayakeerthi understood that Diti was playing a game to provoke him. Struggling to control his displeasure, he said, "I'll order masala dosa," and picked up his phone.

"No need, sir," Varghese said.

"Hey, the masala dosa here is great.

Try it," Diti insisted.

Jayakeerthi ordered the dosa, sensing a deliberate attempt by Diti to stir things up. After they finished the dosa and juice, Varghese stood up,

"Sorry for leaving early. I have some work." "Leaving so soon? You're abandoning me?" Diti asked playfully.

"Unless he's tied to you, how can he abandon you?" Jayakeerthi joked, standing up and shaking Varghese's hand. Varghese extended his hand to Diti, who hugged him and kissed his lips, saying, "Take care!"

Startled by her unexpected behaviour, Varghese hurriedly left without saying a word.

Diti sat down and looked at Jayakeerthi, "Order me a cup of strong coffee."

"What games are you playing with me?" Keerthi asked seriously.

"Why would I play games with you?" Diti raised an eyebrow, a sly smile forming on her lips.

"You know exactly what I mean. Why are you trying to provoke me?" Jayakeerthi demanded, trying to keep his emotions in check. "I'm not provoking you. I'm just living my life. You need to accept that," she said, her tone unwavering. Jayakeerthi clenched his fists under the table, his anger simmering. He knew he needed to approach the situation differently to make any headway.

"Look, Diti, I care about you. I don't want to see you get hurt."

"I can take care of myself, Keerthi. You need to trust me," Diti said firmly. The tension between them was palpable, "Sit down. Didn't I tell you I needed to talk to you privately?" he said, his voice tense with barely suppressed anger.

"Alright, what's it?"

Keerthi stood up, placed both hands on the dining table, and stared at Diti, sitting across from him. "Why did you hug and kiss him? I'm your cousin. How could you do that right in front of me? Don't you have any qualms?" he asked through gritted teeth, his eyes blazing with anger.

"I felt like hugging, so I did. What's the big deal?" Diti stood up, placing her hands firmly on the table, facing Keerthi with determination.

"Who is he for you to hug like that?"

"He's my best friend. I don't need your guidelines on how to behave with him. who are you to question me?"

Diti's voice was loud and clear, her eyes locked onto Keerthi's.

"I'm your cousin, and your future husband," Keerthi shouted.

"Oh, future husband?" Diti burst into laughter, and sat back, her laughter echoing in the room.

Keerthi rushed to her side, lifted her from the chair.

"You spoiled brat," he slapped her hard, shouting.

"You bastard! How dare you slap me?" she screamed, kicking him back with all her strength. She grabbed her bag and stormed out, driving back to her apartment. The force of her kick caused Keerthi's head to hit the wall, and he collapsed to the floor, dazed and in pain.

*** ___ ***

*** ___ ***

"Look, urgently give me a thousand pounds, I need it for bail," demanded Harris from Keerthi, who was sitting at the Restaurant counter on Tuesday morning.

"Come upstairs, we will talk," said Keerthi, leading Harris to his room.

The situation was this: Diti had filed a complaint with the police about the assault on Varghese, but she hadn't mentioned her suspicion of Keerthi's involvement. Based on the CCTV footage from the coffee shop, the police had arrested Robert. Since Paul was not in the footage, he was not apprehended. Harris, having learned about the situation from Paul, visited the police station where Robert threatened to implicate Harris if he didn't get him out of the case. Robert, who had no steady income, survived through petty thefts and minor crimes. The jail was not new to him. Afraid of Robert's threats, Harris had consulted a lawyer who said that Robert could be bailed out for a thousand pounds. Paul had distanced himself from the case, leaving Harris responsible for getting Robert out.

"I told you to make sure this didn't become a police case, didn't I?" Keerthi snapped, his voice sharp with frustration as he closed the door to his room.

"I know, I know. But things got out of hand. Robert's in jail, and he's threatening to implicate me if I don't get him out,".

"How did you let this happen, Harris? This was supposed to be simple!" Keerthi's anger was palpable.

"Look, I need that money to bail Robert out. If he talks, we're all in trouble," Harris insisted, his tone urgent.

Keerthi ran a hand through his hair, frustration bubbling to the surface. "Alright, but this is the last time. You need to make sure he doesn't cause any more trouble," he said, opening a drawer and pulling out a wad of cash. Harris nodded, taking the money.

"I promise, I'll handle it."

Jayakeerthi felt as if the sky had fallen on him as he slumped on the sofa, deep in thought. He realized he should have won Diti over with affection, not force. He shouldn't have involved Harris. Now, he faced losing both his dignity and money with Diti. She was his cousin, and he never imagined things would come to this.

Fine, he thought, from now on, he would handle this delicately. The fault was his. After all this, he decided he couldn't stay in London any longer. He would sell the Restaurant and move to Thanjavur. There, he would manage the college, and the estate, and get into politics. His grandfather had been elected MLA seven times, and with his name, Jayakeerthi believed he could become an MLA too.

Seeing Diti hug and kiss Varghese without any hesitation right in front of him made him realize he didn't want such a frivolous girl. Let her go to ruin, he thought bitterly. He would go to Thanjavur and live as his parents and grandfather wanted. It seemed his aunt wasn't aware of Diti's free-spirited behaviour. He decided he should inform them. If he knew about it and didn't bring it to their attention, it would be wrong, he thought.

After contemplating various scenarios, Jayakeerthi concluded that even if Diti agreed, he shouldn't marry her. The thought of what his life could have been in Thanjavur began to take shape in his mind. He envisioned himself managing the family's properties, leading community projects, and eventually stepping into the political arena, just as his grandfather had done.

In the silence of his room, Jayakeerthi made a firm decision. He would start making arrangements to sell the Restaurant and wrap up his affairs in London. It was time to return to India and carve out a new path for himself, far away from the complications and heartaches of his current situation.

As he began to plan his next steps, a sense of resolve settled over him.

*** --- ***

"Diti, I'm leaving London and going to Thanjavur. I haven't enjoyed living here, and the Restaurant business doesn't suit me. I came here because all of you are here. I wanted to marry you, but it's clear to me now that you don't feel the same way. Trust me, I'm sorry for what happened to Varghese, but that wasn't my intention. Discussing it now will only bring more pain, so let's just forget about it. Please withdraw the complaint you filed with the police. I've already faced enough humiliation and pain. Don't cause me anymore. Please, do me this favour before I leave London,"

Jayakeerthi pleaded, sitting in Diti's apartment, his voice filled with resignation.

"Did you have anything to do with Varghese getting hit?"

"Don't bring that up again. I've already told you it wasn't my intention. It was an unfortunate accident. Let's both forget about it,"

"Alright, since you're saying this, I'll tell my lawyer to withdraw the case. But you don't have to leave London because of me. If you're leaving for your reasons, that's your personal. Just don't trouble me anymore," Diti said firmly, picking up her car keys.

"I need to go to Birmingham now."

*** --- ***

Varghese, who was initially reluctant to file a complaint, had signed it under Diti's insistence. Now, as per Diti's request, he withdrew the complaint. Varghese was naturally innocent and timid. Growing up in poverty, he always kept to himself, away from the affluent environment and people. He didn't know who his father was. When he asked his mother, she said, "I'll tell you when the time comes. Don't ask me again until then." His mother, who worked as a clerk in a church school, had been converted to Christianity by Father Joshua. They had given her a house behind the church school to live in. Varghese, who was bright in his studies, had his education expenses covered by the church. He secured the second rank in his B.E. and joined an MBA program in Bangalore, where he graduated with three gold medals. He got a job at Waves and Waves Software Company through campus placement and worked in their Bangalore office, before being transferred to the London office. He always kept to himself and avoided trouble, found a new experience in Diti's friendship. He was captivated by her courage and straightforwardness. He needed such a protective bond and was delighted with Diti's friendship. With the enthusiasm of youth, he was living in a beautiful world. Sometimes, Diti's behaviour seemed excessive, but he thought she was just being herself. He believed he needed to learn to be fearless like her.

However, not knowing who his father was, Varghese faced ridicule and mockery from his classmates and peers in school. This made him find solace in being alone and away from everyone. When he got a job and moved to Bangalore, he wanted to take his mother along with him, but she refused. When he asked Father Joshua about his father, he said, "We are all God's children; humans are just instruments of God's creation. Don't worry about it." Not wanting to hurt his troubled mother with repeated questions, Varghese accepted his fate and remained silent. Jessica, who was always engaged in church school work and prayers, found her purpose and fulfillment in Ballari's church. Inspired by Mother Teresa, she always wore a white saree and devoted herself to the tasks assigned by Father Joshua, considering them as God's will. She was at peace.

Father Joshua, who had saved her from committing suicide when she was pregnant with an orphaned child, had taken her to the hospital, covered all medical expenses, and provided her with a home and a job. To her, Father Joshua was a living god. Although her son's academic success and high position brought meaning to her life, she was always worried about his marriage.

"Why did you make this sudden decision?" Bhushan asked Jayakeerthi. It was a Sunday morning, and Jayakeerthi was at Dr. Bharati's house for breakfast with Bharati, Bhushan, and Diti. He had informed Bharati the previous day about his visit. It had been a month since the incident with Varghese's police case.

Jayakeerthi glanced at Diti, but she ignored him and focused on her breakfast. "Nothing here is going as I expected. I came to be part of your lives and build mine alongside yours. My expectations have been in vain, so I'm searching for my roots and moving back to Thanjavur," Jayakeerthi explained, his voice filled with resignation.

"Why, Keerthi? We can help you with whatever you need. Stay here with us. I've always told you to stay with us at home, but you chose to stay at your Restaurant. Even now, come and live with us. We have three rooms upstairs; take any room you like," Bhushan offered, his tone sincere.

Bharati endorsed his suggestion and said, "Yes, come and stay here. If you need money for business, I'll provide it. Why are we all here if not to support each other in times of need?" and turning to Diti said," What do you say, Diti?"

"What did you say, Mom?" Diti asked, looking up.

"Keerthi is leaving London and moving to Thanjavur. Did you hear that?"

"So what?" Diti asked, her tone indifferent.

"What do you mean Diti? Doesn't it bother you that he's making such a sudden decision?" Bhushan asked.

Before Diti could respond, Jayakeerthi interjected, "To her, the world is Varghese now. She isn't interested in any others, Auntie."

"Fine, think that Varghese is my world. So what?" Diti retorted, staring at him.

"Should I tell Auntie how much you like Varghese?" Jayakeerthi threatened, his voice rising.

"Fine, you tell her how much I like Varghese, and I'll tell her how much you like Varghese. Deal?" Diti challenged him, her eyes blazing.

Bhushan, who had been silent until now, intervened. "Look, you two, stop this bickering. Let me get straight to the point," he said, turning to Diti. "Keerthi wants to marry you. What's your opinion on that? Tell us now."

Bharati added, "Yes, he expressed this wish to us earlier. If you agree, we have no objections. Let's settle this today. What's your decision?" Jayakeerthi felt relieved that both Bharati and Bhushan supported the idea of their marriage. He looked at Diti, who was taken aback by the serious discussion initiated by her parents. Not wanting to upset them, she remained silent, tapping her spoon lightly on her plate and avoiding eye contact. After a moment of silence, Bharati got up, placed coffee cups in front of everyone, and started sipping her coffee. Diti, however, didn't touch her coffee and stood up.

"I'm going to see my friend," she said, heading towards the stairs.

"Where to?" Bharati called out.

"To London," Diti replied, quickly climbing the stairs to her room. She returned shortly, carrying her bag and car keys. Bhushan, who was standing near the last step, took her bag from her and, holding her by the shoulder, led her back to the chair.

"Look, Diti, you've finished your studies and haven't started working yet. So don't think I'm trying to interfere with your freedom. Tell me, will you marry Keerthi?"

Even though Diti could easily ignore her mother, she couldn't do the same with her father. She had deep admiration for him because he always supported her, fulfilling all her wishes, even when her mother opposed them. When Diti decided to stay in an apartment in London while attending college, her mother strongly opposed it, even taking two days off from the hospital to protest in a way, refusing food and conversation with anyone. Somehow, her father had managed to convince her mother, and Bharati finally agreed with the condition that Diti would come home every weekend for two days. Similarly, Bhushan supported Diti in getting a car despite her mother's reservations.

"I'll look for a job now. Don't bring up the topic of marriage for another four to five years. If I decide to get married, I'll tell you then," Diti replied, her voice steady and resolute.

"No one is rushing to get you married right now, Diti. You can get married whenever you want. We're just asking if you like Keerthi or not," Bharati said, her voice calm but insistent.

This reminded her of how her father, Varadaraja Iyengar, had asked her the same question when arranging her marriage. Bharati's marriage was initially arranged with Dr. Narayan from Coimbatore, but she didn't like it and married Bhushan.

"When the time comes, I'll tell you who I want to marry. Don't force me now," Diti said, her tone firm.

"She seems to like that Christian boy. Let it be, Uncle," Keerthi interjected.

Diti, irritated by his comment, retorted, "Even if I marry John Varghese, it's my choice. But you will never be my choice, remember that" grabbed the car keys from her father's hand and walked out. After the sound of the car faded, Bhushan turned to Keerthi and said, "Sorry about that.

"If you had won her over, it would have been possible. I too broke off my arranged marriage and married Bhushan. Do you think my daughter will marry whoever I tell her to?" Bharati added,

"Alright, Auntie. I've realized she doesn't like me. I did want to marry Diti, but it seems she is very attached to that Christian boy. I believe she will marry him. I told you this so it won't come as a shock if she decides to marry him. That's all," Keerthi said and walked out.

Since it was a Sunday, they had planned to spend the day together and have dinner later. However, Diti and Keerthi had created a tense atmosphere and left abruptly much to the disappointment of Bhushan and Bharati.

"What if Diti does want to marry Varghese, as Keerthi suspects?" Bharati turned to Bhushan and asked, "What do you think?"

"Do you think these kids will listen to us? If she likes him and we say no, will she listen? I think, we don't have any choice but to accept whoever she chooses. What do you think?" Bharati asked Bhushan.

"I won't be happy with it. If she indeed likes him, I'll have to oppose it," and getting up added, "I need some rest. Let's not discuss this matter until she brings it up herself," and walked towards his room. Bharati was surprised by his words.

Jayakeerthi leased out his Restaurant in London and returned to Thanjavur, accompanied by Ramalingam. His departure to London for business had not been well-received by his family, so his return brought joy to his father Lakshmi Narasimha, mother Pankajakshi, and grandfather Varadaraja Iyengar. With twenty acres of paddy fields, a coconut grove, Varadaraja College, and rental properties, they never faced financial difficulties. His father was sixty, his mother fifty-seven, and his grandfather eighty-two. Jayakeerthi's decision to settle in Thanjavur was both a desire and a necessity for them.

Returning from London, Jayakeerthi was a changed man. The humiliation he faced with Diti and the blackmail by Harris over the assault on John Varghese had deeply affected him. Disillusioned, he had decided to follow his father's advice and not engage in any new ventures. His friends upon hearing of his return, visited him and offered various suggestions. Congress leaders encouraged him to lead the Youth Congress. The district Congress president met with his grandfather, urging him to involve Jayakeerthi in politics. Over time, Jayakeerthi became the president of the Youth Congress in Thanjavur district, immersing himself in politics. The Congress party's strategic move to include him, leveraging his family's wealth and his grandfather's popularity, proved beneficial.

Jayakeerthi's days were now filled with political meetings, community events, and strategic planning sessions. He found a new sense of purpose in his political role, channelling his energy into serving the community and building his political career. The support of his family and the respect he garnered from the local community bolstered his confidence.

Despite his newfound focus, the memories of London and the events that transpired there lingered in the back of his mind. He often wondered about Diti and Varghese, but he knew he had to move forward and leave the past behind. His experiences had taught him valuable lessons about resilience, humility, and the importance of making thoughtful decisions.

As he settled into his new life in Thanjavur, Jayakeerthi began to see the potential for growth and positive change in his community. He worked tirelessly to address local issues, improve infrastructure, and support educational initiatives. His dedication and hard work did not go unnoticed, and he quickly became a respected figure in the political landscape of Thanjavur.

*** ___ ***

Within a month of Jayakeerthi leaving London, John Varghese also returned to India. He secured a job at Infosys in Bangalore. Varghese had applied to Infosys and was hired after an online interview, which allowed him to take care of his aging mother.

"Why did you decide to go to India all of a sudden without giving me any hint?" Diti asked Varghese. They were sitting in her apartment on a Saturday evening, the room filled with the comforting aroma of beer and snacks.

"I wanted to tell you after I secured the job. I wasn't sure if I'd get it at Infosys. My mom is getting old, and I need to take care of her," Varghese explained, They were drinking beer and eating chips while chatting.

"So what's your plan after moving to India?" Diti asked, sipping her beer, her curiosity evident.

"I'll rent an apartment near Infosys in Bangalore and have my mom live with me. She has endured hardships throughout her life. I want to make her happy and take good care of her in her final years,"

"You haven't talked much about your family. Can you share a bit if it's okay with you?"
"There's not much to share.

My mom has suffered a lot in her life and raised me under difficult circumstances. She is like a deity to me. I don't know who my father is, and my mom has never told me. Whenever I asked, she would cry, so I stopped asking. When I got the job in London, I didn't want to leave my mom and refused the offer, but Father Joshua insisted, and my mom convinced me to go. I'm very glad now to have a better-paying job at Infosys and to be with my mom again," Varghese said, his voice filled with gratitude and reverence for his mother.

"You don't know anything about your father?".

"I told you, my father passed away before I was born. But I don't know any details about him - what he looked like, his name, what he did for a living, or how he died. My mom raised me as a single mother," Varghese explained.

Diti didn't ask further about his family sensing his discomfort. Despite his background, Diti admired Varghese for his calm and good nature. She didn't see his background as an issue and thought she should meet and talk to his mother someday. After her family brought up the topic of her marriage, Diti started thinking about why she shouldn't marry Varghese. His gentle nature and the fact that he never imposed himself on her made her consider marrying him.

*** ___ ***

Wanting to gauge his feelings indirectly, she invited him over that day. Pushing aside the empty beer bottles, she said, "Shall we have dinner now?"

"What time is it?" Varghese asked, looking at his watch.
"Oh, it's already nine. It's getting late; I should go," he stood up.

"Please, stay here tonight. Who knows when we'll meet again," Verghese hesitated and was quiet for a while before saying, "Alright, let me call Father and inform him," and picked up his mobile. "I'll order chicken biryani for dinner,"

"Oh no, I've never eaten meat. Just some rice and dal will do for me," Varghese protested. "Didn't you have an egg omelet with me that day?"

"Egg is my upper limit," "What kind of Christian are you?" Diti chuckled.

"And what kind of Iyengar are you?" Varghese laughed back. The warmth between them was palpable.

"One moment, I'll call Father and let him know I won't be coming tonight," Varghese said, taking his phone and stepping out of the room. Excited that he was staying the night, Diti picked up the phone and ordered South Indian food for both. The anticipation of spending more time together filled the air, making the evening even more special.

Varghese returned from making his call, confirming that he would stay the night. They sat down to enjoy the meal she had ordered. As they ate, their conversation flowed easily, touching on various topics, from their work experiences to their future aspirations. The warmth of their connection made the evening even more special. After dinner, they settled comfortably in the living room. Diti, feeling a mix of excitement and nervousness, decided it was the right time to talk about her feelings. She turned to Varghese and said, "There's something I've been thinking about for a while now.

I enjoy our time together, and I've come to realize that I care about you deeply."

Varghese looked at her with a warm smile, "Diti, I feel the same way. You've become an important part of my life, and I cherish every moment we spend together."Feeling a sense of relief and joy, Diti continued, "I've been considering the idea of us being more than just friends. I know it's a big step, but I wanted to know if you feel the same." Varghese neared her and held her hand, "Diti, I've been thinking about it too. I believe we could have a wonderful future together.

I'm ready to take that step with you."

Their intimate conversation deepened their bond, and they both felt a sense of certainty about their future together. That night marked the beginning of a new chapter in their relationship, filled with hope and excitement for what lay ahead. They talked late into the night, sharing dreams and plans, feeling closer than ever before.

In the quiet moments, they both understood that this was the start of something truly special.

CHAPTER TWO

ADITI

While Diti was completing the final year of her degree in London, Aditi in Bangalore completed her MBBS and enrolled in a Postgraduate course at M.S. Ramaiah Medical College. Despite being offered a seat in Mysore, Aditi chose to stay in Bangalore, disregarding Bharati's advice to join Mysore.

Calling Aditi Diti's younger sister isn't entirely accurate, considering they were born just a few minutes apart as identical twins. Both were equally beautiful and intelligent, traits they inherited from their mother. While Diti decided to stay with Bharati and Bhushan in London, Aditi chose to live with her aunt and uncle in Bangalore.

When Diti and Aditi were five years old, Bhushan and Bharati visited Bangalore from Birmingham. Anuradha and Nijaguna, who had no children, expressed their desire to adopt one of the twins. Bharati and Bhushan agreed. When asked where they wanted to stay, Aditi, sitting on Anuradha's lap, promptly said she wanted to stay with her.

Anuradha and Nijaguna were both employed at Malleshwaram College, with Anuradha serving as the principal and Nijaguni as a professor. They resided in a modern two-story house on 12th Cross in Malleshwaram, which Anuradha had built after demolishing their ancestral home. The first floor boasted three guest rooms, a mini theatre-style TV room, and a sports room featuring a table tennis table. Aditi had a spacious private room on the second floor, fully equipped with all the necessary amenities for her studies.

Anuradha's parents had passed away due to age-related illnesses, and her brother, who had settled in America as a doctor, had signed over the house to her.

Aditi, excelling in her studies, from her first year in MBBS, had a competitor in Prasad, her classmate. They consistently secured the top two ranks in college, with one always coming first and the other second, never leaving room for anyone else. Naturally, they became close friends.

*** ___ ***

Prasad had passed his PUC with flying colours, scoring a first-class distinction. His father, Arasayya, suggested that he enrolled in TCH (Teacher's Certificate Higher) for one year and become a teacher in the surrounding schools of Hunsur, considering it to be a fortunate and secure path. However, Prasad reminded his father of his earlier encouragement to become a doctor. Arasayya acknowledged this but expressed his concern about the financial burden of such an education.

Kalavati was Prasad's childhood friend and daughter of Javeregowda who had employed Arasayya. When she had heard about Prasad's aspirations, persuaded her father to bear the costs of Prasad's education. Javaregowda, moved by her request, agreed and took Prasad to Bangalore Medical College, paying his fees and ensuring he had all the necessary facilities at the hostel.

Kalavati herself, having found studying science difficult, had joined the J.S.S. Law College in Mysore after her PUC, determined to become a lawyer. She and Prasad made a pact: she would help him if any medical negligence cases were brought against him, and he promised to treat her for free if she ever fell ill. Their childhood friendship had blossomed into a deep bond, one that grew stronger with time despite the societal barriers they faced.

*** ___ ***

"Hello, congratulations on securing the first place in Anatomy and Physiology. My name is Aditi, I'm your classmate," said Aditi, extending her hand to Prasad.

It was their first conversation, and Aditi had approached him in the canteen, her curiosity piqued by the new top scorer.

"Thank you, who doesn't know you? You are the winner of the college beauty contest, right?" Prasad replied, smiling as he shook her hand, "And congratulations on securing Second place in the class."

"Thank you," Aditi said,

"Beauty is not my achievement. But I aimed to be the top scorer in the class, and you surprised me. Shall we go to the nearby Coffee Day for a coffee? I'll treat you," she offered with a playful smile. As they walked towards the Coffee Day across the road in front of the medical college, a sense of camaraderie began to form.

That initial conversation marked the beginning of a close friendship. They frequently studied together, often challenging each other academically, always striving to outdo one another. Their friendly competition pushed them to achieve great heights in their early years of study.

Their bond grew stronger with each passing semester, their mutual respect and admiration forming the foundation of a lasting friendship. Coffee breaks, study sessions, and shared laughter became the highlights of their college life, creating memories that would stay with them forever.

*** ___ ***

"Congratulations, you've finally hit the jackpot," said Prasad, shaking Aditi's hand.

Aditi had passed the final M.B.B.S. exams with distinction, while Prasad, who had passed with first-class honors, missed the distinction by five marks.

"Thanks. What are your plans now?" asked Adit.

"I plan to pursue post-graduation. If I get a seat, I'd like to do an M.S. What about you?" Prasad replied as they sat in their usual spot at Coffee Day which had become their favourite hangout.

"I'm also studying for the PG entrance exam. Will you be studying here or..." she trailed off, leaving the question open-ended.

"No, I'll be studying from our farmhouse in Hunsur."

"Why not stay here and join a coaching class? We can share our studies and help each other. Think about it," Aditi suggested, her eyes lighting up with the idea. "You should visit my home once. Come over for breakfast this Sunday. I'll introduce you to my parents."

"Where is your house?"

"It's the fifth house on the right in the 12th cross, Malleswaram.

The house name is 'Akaran' written in front," Aditi explained. "Why is it named 'Akarana' (For no reason)?"

"I don't know, you can ask my dad, when you come."

"Alright, I'll come. Can you give me your phone number if you don't mind?" Prasad asked, wanting to make sure he could contact her easily.

"Sure," Aditi said, giving him her phone number and saving his on her mobile.

*** ___ ***

"This is my dad, Professor Nijaguna at Malleswaram College," Aditi introduced Nijaguna to Prasad. "This is Prasad, Dad, the most brilliant student in our college," she introduced Prasad to her dad. Although Aditi had not been officially adopted, she affectionately called Nijaguna "Dad" and Anuradha "Mom."

"Hello, Sir. Your daughter, who topped the college and won six gold medals, is giving me undue compliments," said Prasad, shaking Nijaguna's hand with a smile.

"Brilliance is not measured by medals," Nijaguna smiled, "please have a seat." "This is my mom, Anuradha, working as the principal of Malleswaram College."

"Hello, Madam," said Prasad, standing up and folding his hands in greeting.

As promised, Prasad visited Aditi's house that Sunday morning. Anuradha greeted him warmly, "Hello, please have a seat. Aditi mentioned you are from Hunsur. The name Hunsur reminds us of Devaraj Urs. Did you know him?" she asked.

"Knowing in the same way you do, through the media, Madam. After him, one Mr Javaregowda is now MLA of Hunsur constituency. My father manages his land and farms," Prasad replied, his tone respectful.

At that moment, plates of idlis and chutney arrived.

"Please have some breakfast," said Anuradha, heading to the kitchen to prepare coffee.

The three of them chatted while having breakfast. After finishing coffee, Aditi took Prasad to her study room on the second floor. Seeing her well-arranged room, Prasad said, "Your room is perfect for studying," and approached the bookshelf, inspecting the books. "You have all the medical books, impressive,"

"Don't you have just as many books?" she asked.

"I only bought the essential ones. For the rest, I used to sit in the library. I find reading online a hassle, so I haven't bought any software. Can I borrow books from here if needed?"

"Feel free to take any book you need. I have a suggestion, why don't you come here, and we can study together?"

"Will your mom and dad be okay with it?" Prasad asked, a bit hesitant.

"You ask too many questions. My mom and dad support everything that helps my studies. Do you want me to get their approval?" Aditi smiled.

"No, no, I'll come as you suggested. I don't have as many books. It would be convenient for me to come here," From the next day onwards, Prasad started coming to Aditi's house. They spent two to three hours studying and discussing, preparing for the exams, three months away. Their combined efforts and mutual encouragement created a productive and supportive study environment.

"Why not study together," Anuradha suggested, noticing the productive synergy between Prasad and Aditi. Although Prasad usually came over after having dinner at his place, Aditi insisted, "It's better if we have our meals together in our room." She believed it would save time and help them focus more on their studies.

"I appreciate the offer, Aditi, but I prefer to have dinner at my hostel," he said politely.

*** ___ ***

Despite Aditi's insistence, Prasad's decision remained firm. He continued to arrive at Aditi's house after dinner, ready to dedicate a few hours each night to their studies. Their combined efforts and mutual encouragement created an effective and supportive study environment, allowing them to prepare thoroughly for their upcoming examinations

*** ___ ***

"I want to marry Prasad. What do you think?" Aditi suddenly voiced her opinion one morning, causing a startled Anuradha to look at Nijaguna's face. The three of them were having breakfast together. Aditi had finished her postgraduate entrance exams and was waiting for the results. Prasad had gone back to his home in Hunsur.

"Which Prasad?" Nijaguna asked.

"The same, my classmate and the doctor who used to come to our house to study with me."

"Have considered all relevant factors when you made the decisiojn?" Anuradha asked.

"I haven't decided yet, I'm just expressing my feelings. I need your help take this decision" Aditi replied.

"This is a serious matter. We all need to sit down together and discuss it," Nijaguna stated.

"Who all do you mean by 'we all,' Dad?" Aditi asked.

"Bharati, Bhushan, and your grandfather let's all discuss together when they come. They are planning to settle in Bangalore from Birmingham. Bharati has informed me over the phone. Also, Dithi has got a job here in Bangalore. We need to discuss Dithi's marriage as well. If possible, we can plan both marriages together," Anuradha explained.

"Why together?" Aditi asked.

"That's your grandfather's wish. He is already eighty-two years old. Once Bharati, Bhushan, and Dithi come here, let's all go to Tanjavur to visit him. We can discuss the marriage there. What do you say?"

"Okay, Mom. Let's do that. I am happy to know that Dithi got a job here in Bangalore. It's been many years since I saw everyone. And Kirthi has settled in Tanjavur, leaving London. We should visit him as well. Good idea."

*** ___ ***

Diti had secured a job in the Human Resources department at Infosys in Bangalore. Her decision to move to Bangalore was primarily influenced by the need to be with John Varghese.

Before John left London, they had discussed and decided on their marriage during his farewell night, solidifying their commitment to each other.

With Jayakeerthi leaving London and now Diti moving to Bangalore, Bharati and Bhushan started contemplating why they shouldn't also settle in Bangalore. The thought of reuniting with their daughters and being closer to family grew increasingly appealing. They began to weigh the benefits of moving, considering the opportunities and the joy of being surrounded by their loved ones.

The idea of settling in Bangalore started to take shape, and Bharati and Bhushan discussed the potential move more seriously. They envisioned a future where the entire family could thrive together, supporting each other through life's various stages.

The results of the PG entrance exams were out, and both Aditi and Prasad secured ranks within the top 300, giving them the merit to choose any course in any college.

*** ___ ***

"Congratulations! Have you decided which course and where you will choose?" Kalavati asked Prasad.

Kalavati had now completed her LLB, passed the Bar Council exam, registered her name, and started her law practice in Mysore. Javaregowda had bought a three-room apartment on Geetha Road near the court for her. Prasad was visiting her in her apartment on a Sunday morning.

"I want to join the MS course in General Surgery. If I get it, I'll join," Prasad replied confidently.

"With your rank, you'll get it. When is your counselling?"

"On the 25th of August, there are still ten days to go,"

"Alright, assuming you can get a seat in any city, where will you join?" Kalavati inquired further.

"I've decided to join in Bangalore,"

"Why Bangalore? Why not choose Mysore, which is close to home and me?" Kalavati questioned, a hint of disappointment in her voice.

Prasad paused, considering his response carefully.

"Bangalore offers more opportunities and exposure in the field of General Surgery. Plus, Aditi will be there, and we have developed a strong study partnership. I believe it's the best choice for my career growth," he explained.

"Do you love her?" Kalavati asked, looking at Prasad intently, eyes searching for the truth.

"Why are you asking this all of a sudden?" Prasad asked with a smile, trying to deflect the seriousness of the moment.

"Tell me, do you love her? The reason I'm asking is that I've liked you since childhood. I have no hesitation in telling you directly, I want to marry you. What is your opinion on that?" she said, holding both his hands, her voice filled with sincerity.

Prasad, feeling emotional, kissed her hand and said,

"I like you too. But is this possible?" His voice was tinged with uncertainty and hope.

"What do you mean by 'this'?" Kalavati asked.

"Look, there is a huge barrier of caste and status between us. So, is our marriage possible? Your parents will not agree, what do you say?"

Kalavati stood up, embraced him, and said, "If we like each other, then my parents will have to agree. Leave the responsibility of convincing them to me. If you are in love with that classmate, tell me now only."

"No, she is just my best friend. I don't have those feelings for Aditi," Prasad said, his voice reassuring.

Kalavati felt a surge of relief and happiness. She believed in their bond and was determined to overcome any obstacles that stood in their way.

"What is her caste?" Kalavati asked, her curiosity evident.

"I don't know, but looking at their manners and behaviours, I think they must be Brahmins. Whatever the caste, I've never seen her from a marriage perspective.

"No, no, no, this has to be decided now. If you wish to marry me, promise me now," Kalavati insisted, her voice firm and determined.

"Why are you talking like this, Kalavati? Your parents will not agree. Knowing this, how can you think of marrying me?"

"Look, Prasad, I don't believe in castes, and the question of status—there may be a difference in status between our fathers, but not between us, right? I am a lawyer and you are going to be an MS and a renowned surgeon. If you see, your status will be higher than mine," she smiled, trying to lighten the mood.

Prasad, feeling a wave of happiness and relief, embraced her without saying a word. The warmth of the moment conveyed all the emotions and promises they couldn't express in words.

*** ___ ***

As per Kalavati's wish, Prasad joined Mysore Medical College. Attracted to Kalavati since childhood, Prasad had always dreamed of her but believed that due to caste and status differences, it would never happen. He had never expressed his feelings to anyone. Now, with Kalavati herself confessing her love and desire to marry him, a new world of happiness opened up before him, making him elated.

Prasad's focus on his studies remained steadfast, but the prospect of a future with Kalavati added a new dimension to his ambitions.

Meanwhile, Aditi joined the MD (Pediatrics) course at Ramaiah Medical College in Bangalore. One morning, Prasad arrived at Aditi's house with flowers and fruits to bid her farewell. After having coffee, they sat in Aditi's room and talked. Prasad's visits to the house had become a routine, and Nijaguna and Anuradha considered him as one of the family, greeting him with just a "Hi" wherever he arrived. He would go straight to Aditi's room after climbing the stairs.

"I thought you would join here in Bangalore, but you disappointed me by joining in Mysore," Aditi said.

"Sorry, but even though I wanted to join here, I had to join Mysore due to unavoidable circumstances," Prasad was apologetic.

"May I ask what those unavoidable circumstances are?"
Aditi inquired, her curiosity piqued.

"I haven't told you about my background before. I'll tell you now, as we don't know when we'll meet again. My father is the manager of the land owned by Javaregowda, the MLA of Hunsur. We are SCs..."
" How does it matter?" Aditi asked.

"It matters to us in so many ways that you can never imagine"

He was serious, "In a city like Bangalore, caste doesn't matter. Here, what matters is Money. But in villages and towns, relationships and interactions are based on caste. These castes are the malignant diseases of Hinduism. The concept of Dalits or untouchables is more dreadful than leprosy. Your parents probably don't know that I belong to the untouchable category,"

"No, I didn't know. I only knew that my father is a Lingayat and my mother is an Iyengar."

"Of course, some enlightened people have transcended these castes. But if your parents knew that I belong to such a caste, I doubt they would have let me into their house..."

"Please, don't say that. My mom and dad are not like that," Aditi interrupted him.

"Sorry, I didn't mean to speak ill of your parents. These caste calculations consciously affect most of the Hindus and subconsciously influence others. Among Hindus, there are beliefs and practices that one caste is inferior or superior to another. This is a deeply ingrained and harmful tradition that has been practised for thousands of years. It's not easy to break free from its influence. I know this from experience. If I explain further, it will hurt you, so let's leave it at that," Prasad concluded.

CHAPTER THREE

DITI-ADITI

Diti is now in Bangalore, working at Infosys. She chose not to look for a job in London as she wanted to be with John Varghese, and hence applied and secured a position at Infosys.

With their daughter moving to Bangalore and Jayakeerthi already having returned to Thanjavur, Bharati, and Bhushan decided it would be convenient for them to relocate to Bangalore as well. They resigned from their jobs, sold their house, and purchased a luxurious two-storied, five-bedroom house in the fifth block of Jayanagar, Bangalore, relocating their lives there. However, they did not sell the London apartment they had bought for Diti, nor did they rent it out, keeping it for their visits to London.

Now, Bhushan rejoined his old college, National College, as an English professor. Although Bharati had opportunities to join several hospitals in Bangalore, she decided not to join any and chose to live a peaceful, retired life.

They had saved a substantial amount of money from their more than twenty years of work in Birmingham, and even after buying the two crores rupee bungalow, they still had several crores of rupees.

They invested a part of this money in purchasing a tenacre farm with a bungalow in Thanjavur through Bharati's brother Narasimha and deposited a significant amount in the bank through him. Overall, they were financially well-off. Now, Diti is also with them.

*** ___ ***

One Saturday morning, Bharati, Bhushan, and Diti went to Anuradha's house in Malleshwaram. Since they had informed her the previous day, Anuradha had invited them for breakfast and prepared the idli batter and ingredients for making vada the day before.

"So, you have joined Infosys now?" Nijaguna asked Diti.

"Yes, Uncle, they gave me a good offer, so I joined," Diti replied with a smile.

"If you had wanted, you could have gotten a job in London, right?"

Aditi asked, her eyes twinkling with curiosity.

Anuradha, Nijaguna, Bharti, Bhushan, Diti, and Aditi were all seated around the dining table at Anuradha's house, enjoying idli and vada for breakfast. The housemaid was serving them, ensuring everyone had enough on their plates.

"Yes, I could have, but my destiny brought me here," Diti said with a gentle smile, her words filled with a sense of purpose.

"What do you mean by that?" Aditi asked, leaning forward with interest.

"Do you know what Kabir says?"
Diti looked at her, a playful glint in her eyes.

"Who is Kabir, your boyfriend?" Aditi asked, laughing. Everyone present was keenly listening to the intimate talks between the twin sisters. Everyone laughed at Aditi's comment and then looked towards Diti to hear what she would say.

"You silly, don't you know who Kabir is?" Diti teased, her tone lighthearted.

"Well, if you had introduced him, I would have known, right?" Aditi challenged, smiling playfully.

At this point, Nijaguna couldn't contain his laughter and said, "Kabir Das was a great saint of the fifteenth century, dear."

"I didn't know that dad. Okay, so what does your Kabir say?" Aditi turned to Diti and asked, genuinely curious now.

"Let me first tell you who Kabir is, listen. As Uncle said, Kabir Das was a great saint. Not only that, he was a social reformer and a poet. In just two lines, he captured the essence of life. His sayings are popular and beneficial, like our Sarvajna's or the Tamil Thirukkural. Kabir's writings are just two lines, and these are called Dohas, meaning two-line sayings. Kabir is revered by Hindus, Muslims, and Sikhs. Just don't cut corpse, knowing all this is essential, understand?" Diti teased Aditi, her eyes sparkling with mischief.

"Alright, alright, I didn't know. I didn't study religions in college like you did, so I didn't get to know. Anyway, now tell me what your Kabir says?" Aditi asked with a soft smile.

"'Dane dane par likha hai khane wale ka naam' is one of Kabir's sayings," Diti replied, her eyes twinkling with knowledge.

"What does that mean?" Aditi asked.

"Kabir says that every grain has the name of the person who will eat it written on it, did you know?" Diti explained. As Aditi picked up a vada from Diti's plate and put it in her mouth, she said, "Look, I ate the vada that you were supposed to eat. Doesn't that contradict Kabir's saying?" she laughed, her eyes gleaming with mischief.

"Oh, silly, your name was written on it, which is why I couldn't get it even though it was on my plate, did you know?" Diti said seriously.

The room filled with laughter as everyone appreciated the humorous and affectionate exchange between the sisters. Anuradha and Nijaguna exchanged amused glances, while Bharti and Bhushan smiled warmly, cherishing the close bond their daughters shared. The conversation not only enlightened everyone about Kabir's teachings but also added a layer of warmth and joy to their breakfast gathering.

"What Diti is saying is true, dear, your name was on it," Nijaguna added.

"Alright then, since you both are saying it, I have to accept it. Now tell me, how does that saying relate to you leaving London and getting a job in Bangalore?"

"You will understand it slowly in the coming days, don't rush," Diti replied with a knowing smile. She then turned to Anuradha and asked, "Aunty, is there coffee?"

"It's coming," said Anuradha, and the housemaid brought coffee for everyone.

Diti's cryptic words were not fully understood by Anuradha and Nijaguna, who exchanged puzzled looks. Bharti and Bhushan, however, strongly suspected it had something to do with Varghese and exchanged meaningful glances.

After breakfast, Diti and Aditi went to the TV room on the first floor. Anuradha and Bharti sat on chairs under the tree in the backyard, engaged in conversation, while Bhushan and Nijaguna walked towards Bhashyam Park.

"What do you mean by your words?" Aditi asked Diti. The two of them were sitting on the sofa in the TV room, not seriously watching the movie that was playing.

"Have you ever loved anyone?" Diti asked Aditi.

"Yes, how did you know?" Aditi asked in surprise.

"Did you forget that we are twins? That's why I asked," Diti smiled softly.

"In that case, you must also love someone. Who is it?" Aditi asked, her curiosity growing.

Diti shared about her friendship with John Varghese and said, "I am going to marry him."

"Are you saying he is a Christian? Do you think our elders will agree?"

"That can be dealt with later; now tell me, who is the guy you love?"

Diti asked, steering the conversation back to her.

"Like you, my love is also complicated," Aditi laughed, a touch of irony in her voice.

"What do you mean?" Diti asked, intrigued.

Aditi told her about Prasad, the guy she loved, "He is very intelligent and a good person. But he says he belongs to the untouchable caste. You have studied religions, can you explain what it means to be untouchable?" Aditi asked, her voice tinged with confusion and curiosity.

"Your case is even more complicated than mine. Let me explain what untouchables are," Diti said, and then explained the concept of the four varnas, and finally, about the fifth group, the Panchamas, who have been subjected to oppression for thousands of years. She also mentioned the Manusmriti and Dr. B.R. Ambedkar's works.

"Even if our parents agree to the marriage with that boy, Grandfather will never agree to this marriage. Anyway, have you told him about your wish?"

"Not yet; but I have told Mom and Dad once,"

"Did you tell them about the boy's caste?"

"No."

"Why not?"

"At that time, I didn't know about his caste."

"Can I give you some advice?"

"Sure, what is it?"

"First, talk to that boy and make sure he likes you. If he does, we can discuss this further," she advised.

"You're right, but I will soon be joining my PG course, which will be another three years of study. So even if he agrees, we will have to wait three more years to get married,"

"That's all for later. First, find out his opinion. You shouldn't have brought this up with Mom and Dad without knowing that," Diti insisted, her tone firm.

"And have you asked your boy's opinion?"

"Yes, we both like each other. Though he hesitated initially, he eventually agreed," Diti replied, a smile playing on her lips.

"Why did he hesitate?"

"He thought our family wouldn't accept him," Diti explained.

"What is his concern?"

"Firstly, status. He comes from a lower-middle-class family. His mother is a teacher at a church school. He doesn't know who his father is, and they are Christians," "Even then you will marry him?"

"I will, because he matters to me, not his background. His goodness has won me over. Besides, we both have good jobs. What more do I need? This is enough for me. Now, about Grandfather. He is oldfashioned. It might be challenging to convince him. Let's see," Diti said, her determination clear.

"What will you do if he doesn't agree?"

"I will cross the bridge when I come to it," Diti laughed, her optimism shining.

*** __ ***

Meanwhile, Bhushan and Nijaguna were sitting in the park, discussing.

"I am happy that you came to Bangalore from Birmingham. Having you here is good company for me. You should often come here on with Bharati," said Nijaguna, his tone filled with warmth.

"I've always wanted to come and settle in Bangalore. Now that Diti has completed her education and got a job here, it gave us a reason to move. Where is Ganapathi now?" Bhushan asked, referring to their youngest brother.

"He is currently an SP in Bidar. He comes home and talks to us whenever he has any duty in Bangalore," Nijaguna replied.

"Why did Jayakeerthi leave London? Did he face any losses in business?"

"Nothing like that. He just got bored and left. Moreover, he is already twenty-eight years old. It's time for him to get married. He must have thought it would be easier to get married while being in Thanjavur than in London. He once mentioned to us that he wanted to marry Diti. But Diti didn't like him," Bhushan explained, his tone matter-of-fact.

"Why? What did she find lacking in him?"

"Only God knows," Bhushan chuckled, shaking his head.

"Is she in love with someone else?" Nijaguna asked.

Bhushan hesitated for a moment, wondering whether to share or not, then decided it was best to be open, and told him about Diti and John Varghese.

He mentioned that she had been very friendly with John and might even wish to marry him.

"Has she said so to you?"

"Not yet. But the fact that the boy got a job at Infosys and she came here instead of exploring opportunities in London makes me think she came here looking for him," Bhushan explained.

After sitting in silence for a while, Nijaguna asked, "Have you both discussed what to do if she decides to marry him?"

"We have talked about it casually. If she explicitly says she wants to marry him, then we need to discuss it. I'll contact you then. Have you thought about Aditi's marriage?" Bhushan asked.

"I called you to the park mainly to discuss her," said Nijaguna, causing Bhushan to become anxious.

"What's the matter?"

"She once mentioned wanting to marry a boy named Dr. Prasad, who was her classmate,"

"Do you know his background?"

"He has been her classmate since the first year of M.B.B.S. He used to come to our house and study with Aditi for the PG entrance exams. But I don't know what his background is. We thought she might have said it impulsively. We are staying quiet, thinking we will investigate if she seriously brings it up again. You also shouldn't bring this topic up in front of her," Nijaguna advised.

*** ___ ***

Anuradha's phone rang, and she picked it up.

"Hello Anu, it's Narasimha from Thanjavur,"

"Hello, Narasimha, how are you all?"

"We are all fine here. How is everyone there?"

"Everyone here is fine too. How is Uncle?"

"I called to talk about him," said Narasimha, as Anuradha continued, "He should be around eighty-one years old now, right?"

"He turned eighty-two last September; he is now eighty-three. His BP and sugar levels have increased, so we have admitted him to the local Annapurna Nursing Home. He said he wanted to see all of you, so I called," "Oh, is it serious?"

"Not really. He will be discharged tomorrow. His BP and sugar levels are now under control. There's no need to worry," Narasimha reassured her.

"Did you call Bharati?" Anuradha asked.

"No, I called you first. I'll call her now. If you all could come and visit him for a couple of days, he would be very happy. Talk to Bharati and the others and call me," "Alright, I'll talk to them. You inform Bharati," said Anuradha, and hung up the phone.

*** ___ ***

Come here, Aditi, where is Diti?"
Varadaraj Iyengar asked, holding Diti's hand.

"Grandpa, I am Diti. Aditi is inside; she will be here soon." Diti replied, Just then, Aditi came over and held his hand, saying, "How are you, Grandpa?"

Now they were in Tanjavur. One by one, everyone came to the hall where Varadaraj was seated. Lakshmi, sister of Jayakeerti who was pursuing her Post Graduation in medicine at Grants Medical College was also there. Everyone had finished their breakfast. Pankajakshi had joyfully prepared idli-vada, sweet and savoury Pongal, and dosa with chutney and potato palya. Anuradha and Bharati had joined her. The three of them had prepared four types of chutney, chutney powder, and okra sambar. After a grand breakfast and filtered coffee, everyone came to the hall one by one. Varadaraj was sitting on the sofa. It had been a week since he was discharged from the hospital. Around six feet tall and once a yoga master, his robust body now showed the signs of ageing and illness. If not for diabetes and blood pressure, he wouldn't have become so frail and bedridden. For many years, he had been taking insulin injections, and his body seemed to be dependent on them.

Diti and Aditi sat to his left and right. They had placed chairs from the dining table in front of the sofa to provide seats for everyone.

"Is everyone here, Narasimha?" Varadaraj asked his son.

"Yes Dad, everyone is here and seated," Narasimha replied.

Varadaraj's wife, Lalithamma, had passed away ten years ago.

"Due to diabetes, my vision has become blurry, and it's difficult to recognise people from a distance. Therefore, it would make me happy if you all could come closer, hold my hand, and talk to me," Varadaraj said.

"Uncle, I am Anuradha from Bangalore," Anuradha said, sitting next to him and holding his hand.

"Dear Anu, how are you?" he asked warmly, pressing her hand. Anuradha was the daughter of Varadaraj's elder brother, Sampath Iyengar.

"I'm fine, Uncle, with your blessings," Anuradha replied.

"Everything is His will, dear. We humans have no control. We must play our parts as He directs us. By the way, isn't Nijaguna here?" he asked.

"I'm right here, Sir," Nijaguna said, approaching and holding his hand.

"How are you, Master? Are you still in service?" he asked, pressing his hand.

"Yes, I still have five more years of service, and Anuradha has seven more years. We are both at Malleshwaram College," Nijaguna replied.

"Good, it's all His will. I am glad you made time to come. May God keep you well. Is Bhushan here?" Varadaraj asked.

"I am right here, Sir," Bhushan said, approaching and sitting beside him. Bharati sat on his left side.

"I am Bharti, please don't strain yourself, Dad, " she said, holding his hand.

"Narasimha told me you have all moved to Bangalore. Is everything convenient?" Varadaraj asked, patting her head.

"Everything is convenient, no problems at all."

"Are you staying in a rented house or...?"

"No Dad, we bought our own house," Bharati replied.

"That's good to hear. How did you manage the money?" he turned to his son and asked, "Narasimha, you didn't tell me they bought the house?"

"I thought I did, Dad," "Buying a house in Bangalore is no small feat; it must have cost crores of rupees. How much money did you give your sister to buy the house?"

Narasimha scratched his head and turned to Bharati, who hadn't received a rupee from him.

"We had enough savings from our earnings, Dad. If I needed to, I would have asked Narasimha for help without hesitation," Bharati explained.

"Look, dear, this is not a matter of necessity. It's the first responsibility of a father to ensure his daughter has a nice house and lives comfortably. After that, it's her husband's responsibility," Varadaraj said, turning to Narasimha. "Transfer fifty lakhs to her account."

"It's not necessary, Dad. I will ask when I need," Bharati said, kissing his forehead and returning to her seat.

At that moment, Pankajakshi brought and served everyone some fresh orange juice. Since Varadaraj was diabetic, he wasn't given juice. Instead, he was served a glass of ginger decoction. For a while, everyone engaged in quiet conversations.

"One moment, may I have everyone's attention, please," Varadaraj said, making everyone fall silent and look at him.

"My journey in life is coming to an end..."

"Please don't say that, dad..." Bharati interrupted him, "Listen, I know what is happening to me very well. This is reality. If everyone who is born were to live forever, the earth would one day have no space for people to set foot on," he said, calling Bharti closer and holding her hand.

"Have you seen the movie 'Troy,' the story of Helen?" he asked.

"Yes, I have watched it twice, it's an amazing movie," Bharati replied, curious and surprised as to why he suddenly remembered that movie.

"In that movie, there is a dialogue by one of the characters that still resonates with me. Do you know which one?"

"Which dialogue, Dad?"

As the conversation veered in an unexpected direction, everyone there grew curious and eagerly awaited his next words.

"The Gods envy us, the Men, because we are mortal, unlike them. We can die at any moment, while they cannot. That is their lament. Do you see the curse of immortality?" he laughed.

The topic was serious, so no one else laughed.

"Please listen without feeling disheartened," he looked around at everyone.

"What is it, dad?" Bharati asked.

"Bhushan, Nijaguna, Anuradha, please listen carefully," "Alright, what is it, Uncle?" Anuradha asked.

He turned towards Diti and Aditi and said, "I want to ask for one of these beautiful girls' hands in marriage for my grandson Jayakeerthi,"

Upon hearing this, Diti and Aditi got up and walked out towards the garden in the yard. Anuradha, Nijaguna, Bharati, and Bhushan exchanged glances, unsure who should speak or what to say, creating an uneasy atmosphere.

"If they like each other, we have no objections," Anuradha said, looking at Bharati.

"Yes, I also wish the same. If either Diti or Aditi likes Jayakeerthi, we will certainly arrange their marriage; this is our promise,"

Bharati assured, holding Varadaraj's hand.

"Yes, we agree with that too," Anuradha added.

Before leaving Thanjavur, Jayakeerthi had asked Diti,

"What do you say to Grandpa's proposal?" "My marriage is already decided. Knowing this, why are you asking?"

*** ___ ***

Sometimes, on weekends, Diti would go on trips with Varghese to places like Bandipur or B. R. Hills, leaving on Friday evenings and returning home by Sunday evening. This behaviour worried Bharati and one Sunday morning, she asked Bhushan, "How do you interpret her behaviour?"

"She hasn't told me anything. Has she told you?" Bhushan asked, his brows furrowed with concern.

"The last time, as she was leaving for the office, she said, 'I won't be home tonight, going to Bandipur with Varghese. I'll be back on Sunday night,' and left with a kit and her office bag without waiting for my response. This Friday, she said, 'We're going to B. R. Hills, back on Sunday,' and drove off. Her friendship with John Varghese has gone too far. What should we do?"

"Her free-spirited behaviour is not right. However, we must handle this delicately. Let's talk to her when she comes home this evening," Bhushan suggested, trying to maintain a calm approach.

When Diti returned home on Sunday evening and they sat around the dining table, Bharati asked,

"Can I ask why you go out with Varghese and spend two or three days with him?"

"He is the one I am going to marry. That's why we go together," Diti replied, her tone steady.

"Then you could have discussed this with us, right?" Bhushan said, his voice reflecting both surprise and concern.

"Alright, I am telling you now, John Varghese and I have decided to get married. I assumed you would agree, right?" Diti asked, looking at them earnestly.

"Is this decision solely yours, or...?" Bhushan began, trying to understand the situation.

"It is our decision. I was waiting for the right time to tell you. It's good that you brought it up now,"

"Listen, Diti, we are your parents, not your enemies. Making such a unilateral decision about a significant milestone in your life without discussing it with us is not right," Bharati said with pain in her voice.

"Mom, I have been thinking of discussing this with you. Please give me your consent and support our marriage,"

"But have you forgotten what your grandfather said in Thanjavur?" Bharati asked.

"What did he say?"

"He expressed his wish to marry you to Jayakeerthi in front of all," Bharati reminded her.

"He didn't specifically mention my name, did he?" Diti countered.

"Alright, let's assume he specifically asked for you. Even Jayakeerthi had expressed his wish to marry you when he visited our house in Birmingham. Now, with your grandfather's wish, why can't you marry Jayakeerthi? If you agree to marry him, we will also be pleased. So, think about it," Bharati urged.

"My marriage has already been decided, and there is no question of reconsidering," Diti said decisively.

"Alright, we need to talk to the boy. Invite him over for breakfast on Sunday morning," Bhushan said before Bharati could speak.

"Sure, Daddy, thank you," Diti replied, feeling a mix of relief and anticipation.

*** ___ ***

"Do you want to marry Diti?" Bhushan asked John Varghese. John, taken aback, turned to Diti for support.

That Sunday morning, Varghese had come to Bhushan and Bharati's house in Jayanagar at Diti's invitation. After everyone had breakfast and coffee, Bhushan asked this pointed question.

"I've already told you, Daddy, this is a mutual decision between us," Diti said, trying to support Varghese.

"Look, your father is asking him a question. Let him answer; don't interrupt," Bharati said with a hint of irritation.

"Alright, tell us your decision," Bhushan said to Varghese, crossing his legs, resting his hands on his lap while looking at him encouragingly.

"Yes, Uncle," Varghese said nervously, wiping his face with a handkerchief. He was visibly sweating.

"Why do you like Diti?" Bharti asked, looking at Varghese intently.

"Mom, I already told you that we like each other and want to be together for life. him and he me," Diti interjected.

"Look, we are asking him some questions for clarification. You shouldn't interrupt. If you can't stay quiet, go outside for a while," Bhushan said.

"Sorry, Daddy, I'll be upstairs in my room. Call me when you need me," Diti said, giving Varghese a thumbs-up for encouragement before heading to her room.

"Tell us, why do you like Diti?" Bhushan asked again, focusing on Varghese.

"Excuse me," Varghese said, pouring water into the glass on the table and drinking it nervously. "Uncle, this decision is primarily Diti's," he stammered.

"So, you don't have any reasons of your own?" Bhushan asked sharply.

"Her wish is my wish, Uncle," Varghese replied, his voice shaky.

"Have you discussed this with your mother?" Bharati asked.

"No, Aunty," Varghese answered quickly.

"Alright, first discuss this with your mother. After knowing her opinion and if she agrees, we can talk again," Bharati said, turning to Bhushan. "What do you think?" she asked.

"That's correct. First, talk to your mother," Bhushan agreed with Bharati's suggestion, feeling the need for more clarity and approval from Varghese's side.

*** ___ ***

The next day during the lunch break at the office, Diti and Varghese were sitting in a corner of the Infosys canteen when Diti asked,

"You still haven't told your mother about this, have you?"

"No."

"Why?"

"Why, I don't understand myself," he gave a feeble smile.

"Do one thing," Diti suggested.

"What?"

"After office today, I'll accompany you to your house."

"And then?"

"We'll tell Auntie about our decision together," Diti proposed. Varghese remained silent, contemplating her suggestion.

"Don't be scared. I'll bring up the topic," she encouraged him.

*** ___ ***

That Sunday morning, Bharati and Bhushan accepted Varghese's invitation and went to his house for breakfast with Diti. Having received Jessica's blessings, Varghese had invited them for talks.

As they entered his apartment on the second floor, they saw a small statue of Jesus Christ and a large photo of Mother Mary in the showcase on the front wall. As they moved forward and turned right, they saw a sofa, a TV, and a dining table facing the kitchen. A painting of "The Last Supper" hung on the wall above the dining table.

Varghese's mother, Jessica, welcomed them, seated them on chairs, and served them coffee in cups and saucers, placing a plate of chips on the coffee table. Jessica was thin and fair. She must have been over fifty years old, but the wrinkles on her cheeks made her look like she could be sixty. There were white hairs at the edges of her hairline. Her face had a calm expression, with a gentle smile.

"You all talk, we'll go to the shop and get some groceries and vegetables,"

Diti and Varghese said as they left.

"Is the shop far?" Bharati asked.

"It's about three kilometres away; they'll go by car," Jessica replied. Varghese had bought a car with a bank loan to commute to the office.

"Our Diti loves your son and wants to marry him," Bharati began the conversation, her tone straightforward.

"They both have told me that," Jessica said.

"Do you approve of this?" Bharati asked, her eyes searching Jessica's face for any sign of resistance.

"We are poor, and you are wealthy. There is a significant difference in our statuses. So, this matter is up to you," Jessica said, her voice humble.

"You are Christians, and our daughter is Hindu. Do you see any issue with these religions?" Bhushan asked, probing gently.

"I was originally Hindu. After my husband passed away, I converted to Christianity for my son's sake. In my view, there is no difference between Christianity and Basava Dharma. Basavanna's principles of 'Do not steal, do not kill' are similar to Jesus Christ's principle of 'If someone strikes you on the right cheek, turn to him the other also,' right?" she smiled, trying to draw a connection.

"Your comparison is accurate. May I ask how you became familiar with Basava Dharma?" Bhushan asked.

At that moment, Bharti said, "Excuse me for a minute, I need to use the restroom," Jessica got up to show her the way.

"What did you ask?" Jessica asked as she returned and sat down.

"I asked how you became familiar with Basava Dharma." " Basically I belong to the Lingayat sect of Hinduism. Though I changed my religion, I haven't abandoned the Lingayat traditions. Both Varghese and I are vegetarians. Occasionally, we boil eggs and make omelettes at home," she smiled, trying to ease the atmosphere.

"Also, Varghese once told me when he visited our house in Birmingham that you used to work at a printing press in Bellary.

Is that true?" Bhushan asked, his tone cautious. This question unsettled Jessica.

"Yes, I have left all that behind and become a new person. Remembering those days brings me pain. Please forgive me," she said, standing up.

"Sorry, please sit down. The reason is that I am also from Kottur, and my elder brother used to work at a printing press in Bellary a long time ago. I was curious if you might have known him," Bhushan explained, trying to calm her.

"Really?" Jessica said, sitting down again. "Which printing press was he working at?" she asked.

"He worked at the press owned by freedom fighter Shantarudrappa. My brother once told me that," Bhushan replied.

"What was his name?"

"Bhadrappa. Did you know him?" Bhushan asked.

"Did he die in a railway accident?"

"Yes, how do you know that?"
Bhushan asked, his curiosity deepening.

"Is your elder brother a lecturer at a college in Bangalore?"

"Yes, you must have learned it through Diti," Bhushan said, trying to piece things together.

"Oh! My God, no!" Jessica got up and said, "Sorry, this marriage cannot happen. You should keep your daughter away from my son,and we need never discuss this again,"

"May I know why?" bewildered, he asked,

"My son and your daughter are siblings, No more discussions please," Jessica said just as Bharati emerged from the restroom and heard her words.

*** ___ ***

"Congratulations," Aditi said, shaking Prasad's hand warmly.

"Congratulations to you too! I got the 287th rank. What about you?" Prasad asked, smiling.

"I got the 299th rank. What course do you plan to choose next?"

Aditi inquired; her curiosity piqued.

"I am interested in Surgery, so I plan to choose MS in Surgery.

Meanwhile, I have received a placement offer from a hospital in the USA," Prasad replied.

"Are you going to join there?"

"No, I'll join PG here,"

"Why? Many doctors consider it lucky to get a job in the USA,"

"True, but my parents are not willing for me to go so far away from them. I don't have the heart to leave them either. Anyway, which course will you choose?" Prasad asked, shifting the focus.

"I haven't decided yet."

"Why not?"

"I'm considering whether to choose OBG or Pediatrics," "Didn't you previously say you were going to choose OBG?" Prasad asked, trying to understand her dilemma.

"Yes, I did. But my mom suggested Pediatrics is more suitable for me, saying it focuses on child health. She says doing OBG would make it difficult to find time. There would be emergencies throughout life, many times one had to get up in the middle of the night. Life would be spent in delivery rooms and surgeries, my mom says" Aditi explained.

"Excuse me, your mother is a lecturer, right?"

"Oh, I forgot to mention," Aditi laughed, "My birth mother is Dr. Bharati. She served for twenty years in a hospital in Birmingham and is now settled in Bangalore. Anuradha is my aunt who adopted me and raised me from the day I was five years old. I didn't have the chance to tell you this before."

"You are truly fortunate," Prasad remarked, his voice filled with admiration.

"Why?"

"God has given you two mothers to take care of you,"
Prasad smiled, his eyes twinkling.

"That's true," Aditi smiled. "Are you joining here in Bangalore?"

"No, I will choose Mysore Medical College," "Why Mysore? Why not join here in Bangalore?"

"Let me tell you about my background,"

"What is it?" Aditi asked her attention fully on him.

"Hunsur is my hometown. We are Dalits, meaning the Hindu society considers us untouchable. I have mentioned this to you before. Let me tell you again. My father works for Javaregowda, the MLA of Hunsur, managing his lands and farms. Javaregowda has been covering the expenses for my education. His daughter, Kalavati, and I have been friends since childhood. She is a lawyer in Mysore. We have been in love since childhood and have decided to get married. That's why I am joining Mysore Medical College," Prasad explained, his voice filled with emotion. Hearing his words, Aditi was taken aback.

"That's why they say 'Man proposes, God disposes,'" she said with a smile.

"What do you mean ?"

"Nothing, just wishing you all the best. Whatever happens, don't give up on your love," Aditi advised, her voice gentle.

"I don't know why you are saying this, but our marriage won't be that easy,"

"Why? What is the problem?" Aditi asked, curious. After a moment of silence,

Prasad sighed and said, "The difference in caste and status is as vast as the earth and the sky. I fear Kalavati's parents will never agree to this marriage. But Kalavati is a determined and courageous girl. We will have to wait and see what happens."

"May your love overcome all obstacles and succeed. Keep in touch and call me often. Meet me whenever you come to Bangalore," Aditi concluded.

*** ___ ***

"Hello, Daddy?" Kalavati answered her ringing mobile on that Friday night, realizing it was her father, Javaregowda.

"Hello, Kala, how are you, dear?" Javaregowda asked, his voice warm.

"I am doing well, Daddy. How are you all? Is Mom doing well?"

"Everything is fine. I wanted to discuss something important with you,"

"What is it?" Kalavati asked, curiosity evident in her voice.

"Do you have court tomorrow, Saturday?"

"I have one hearing in the morning. No cases in the afternoon. Why do you ask?"

"Come to Hunsur by tomorrow evening," "Why, Dad? What's special?"

"I'll tell you when you come," he said and hung up the phone.
"Your father has called you over to discuss your marriage,"
Kalavati's mother, Jayamma, said, serving her coffee.

"What do you mean? Please explain, Mom," Kalavati replied,
confused and slightly apprehensive.

"Tomorrow, a suitor's family is coming from Bangalore to see you.
That's why your father has called you," Jayamma explained. Just
then, Javaregowda came downstairs.

"Yes, dear. Tomorrow morning, an IAS officer is coming with his
parents to see you. He is the Commissioner of the Housing Board in
Bangalore. His father, MLA Siddhegowda, is an old friend of mine.
That's why I have called you," he said, pulling a chair at the dining
table and asking his wife, "Give me a cup of strong coffee, too."
Jayamma entered the kitchen.

"You should have told me this when you called," Kalavati said.

"Why?"

"If I had known, I wouldn't have come,"

"Why? What's the problem?

You are already twenty-three years old. How much longer do you
want to stay single?"

"That's not the issue. My marriage, my life, my choice. I won't
accept anyone, not even God, imposing it on me. I understand
you are doing this as a fatherly duty. But summoning me without
informing me about it feels oppressive. I am leaving for Mysore
right now," she said, slamming her coffee cup on the table and
standing up.

"Remember who you are talking to" Javaregowda shouted, standing up and walking towards her.

Sensing the situation escalating, Jayamma intervened,

"You stay quiet. I will talk to her,"

"Do what you want, but if she leaves for Mysore today, she need not come back to this house ever again," Javaregowda thundered as he left the house, instructing the driver to drive to the local guest house and getting into the car.

Kalavati didn't return to Mysore that day. Although she was upset by her father's stern words, she decided to stay back in Hunsur and resolve the matter.

*** --- ***

The next morning at ten o'clock, the suitor's family from Bangalore arrived at Javaregowda's house. After breakfast and coffee, Kalavati, prepared for the meeting, sat on the sofa beside her mother.

"May I ask why you chose the legal profession?" the IAS suitor asked, sitting on the sofa opposite her with his parents.

"You may ask," Kalavati said.

The suitor, somewhat taken aback, laughed softly, "Alright, tell me, why did you become a lawyer?"

Kalavati crossed her legs and leaned forward, "Excuse me, I don't understand why you are asking this question,"

"Just out of curiosity. You see, the reason I chose to become an IAS officer was to secure a high position in the government and ensure a safe and prosperous life. Similarly, there must be some inspiration or reason for you to choose this profession, right?"

"What you say and ask is natural. My father wanted me to become a doctor. But I chose this profession because, instead of focusing on the fleeting health of this body, I wanted to fight against the inequalities and oppressions in society," she explained, her eyes reflecting her determination.

"What inequalities do you wish to fight against?"

"All inequalities, such as caste hierarchies, the disparity between rich and poor, the oppression in a male-dominated society, exploitation in the name of religion. Our society is full of injustices. I became a lawyer to fight against all these oppressions and to stand for justice and equality," Kalavati spoke with firm conviction and a hint of passion.

The young man, taken aback by her strong words glanced at his father. Clearing his throat, the suitor's father said, "Look, all this is beyond our expectations. The social justice you talk about might be valid. But more important to us is your personal and family life. My son is an IAS officer, and like your father, I am also an MLA. We have enough wealth to last for generations. I have only one son. If you stay with him and manage the household, that is more than enough for us. Why burden yourself with going to court? Living comfortably at home is enough. This is our collective opinion," he said, turning to Javaregowda. "What do you say, Gowdare?" he asked.

"What else can I say, Sir? We want our children to be happy. Whether it's my daughter or your son, there's no need for them to work for money. They can do what they like. In this regard, my opinion is that it is her right and freedom to decide whether to continue in the legal profession. We should not obstruct it,"

Javaregowda said, supporting his daughter.

"I don't want to lose my freedom for any reason. I will continue in my profession." Kalavati emphasised.

The suitor, taken aback by her words, asked, "May I know what hobbies you have, if any?"

"Occasionally, I go to our lawyers' club and play cards. Sometimes, I drink beer, but I don't smoke cigarettes," Kalavati said confidently, crossing her legs and looking at him as if to say, 'What of it?'

"Why don't you smoke cigarettes?" the suitor's father asked, trying to hide his disappointment.

"I tried, but I couldn't continue because of throat irritation and coughing,"

Her response made them turn to look at Javaregowda.

"Hehe... she's just joking," Javaregowda laughed heartily, trying to diffuse the tension.

The suitor looked questioningly at Kalavati again.

"If you think you came here for a joke, take my words as a joke too. I need to go to the restroom," she said, standing up and walking towards her room, leaving the suitor and his family in silence.

"What have you done?" Javaregowda scolded his daughter after the guests had left, his voice filled with frustration.

"What do you mean?" Kalavati asked, her tone steady and calm.

"If you speak like that in front of the guests, what happens to my honour?" he asked angrily, his face flushed.

"I just told the truth, that's all," she said, adding, "I'm leaving for Mysore now. I have an important case in court tomorrow, and I need to prepare for it."

Without waiting for a response, she picked up her car keys and bag and left.

Her parents sat down, bewildered and unsure of what to do next.

*** ___ ***

"Did you understand what she meant?" Bhushan asked Bharati that night before going to bed after dinner.

"No, I didn't. I heard her say, 'My son and your daughter are siblings,' but I didn't understand how. Did you?"

"At first, I too didn't understand either. But slowly, when I thought about it, I think this might be the case," Bhushan said, his voice thoughtful.

"What?"

"My elder brother, Bhadrappa, was in Bellary about thirty years ago, working at a printing press. He died in a railway accident. At that time, I was in Thanjavur and had no contact with anyone. This is what I heard from my elder brother. As far as we know, he was not married. But now, after hearing Varghese's mother, I think my brother Bhadrappa might be Varghese's father. However, she didn't explicitly say it. I am contemplating, should we discuss this with my elder brother?" Bhushan looked at Bharati, his expression serious.

"This is indeed surprising. London is so far from Bellary, and what we know of Varghese is nowhere near what you're suggesting. This is a dramatic twist. That's why they say, 'Truth is stranger than fiction,‘ Bharati said after a moment of astonished silence.

"We shouldn't be the ones to tell Diti about this. Let Varghese's mother handle it," and added. "What do you think?"

“You are right, ” He said.

*** ___ ***

"What happened at Varghese's house yesterday while Varghese and I were out? When We returned everyone was already home. What did you talk about with Varghese's mother, Mom?" Diti asked Bharati. It was Monday evening, and Diti was having coffee after returning from the office. Bhushan was also there, having coffee with her.

"I didn't talk much with her. Your dad and his mother talked. Ask him," Bharati replied.

Diti turned to Bhushan.

"I shared my background, and she talked about her struggles. It was all formal conversation," Bhushan said.

"No, there must have been some serious discussion," Diti insisted.

"Why do you think so?"

"Because today, Varghese told me, we shouldn't see each other anymore. Not only that, but he also said his mother is against this marriage. Initially, she agreed, but now, after meeting you, she is against it. Common sense says it must be because of your conversation. Tell me the truth, Daddy. If you had told me directly that you didn't approve, I might have agreed and stayed away from Varghese. But you shouldn't have deceived me like this," Diti said with tears.

Bharati moved closer and sat beside her. Diti buried her face in Bharati's lap and cried harder. Bharti gently stroked her head without saying anything. Bhushan also remained silent. After a while, Diti, who had soaked Bharati's lap with her tears, suddenly stood up and said, "Sorry..." and went to the bathroom to wash her face. She returned and sat beside Bhushan, holding his hand tightly.The three of them remained silent for a while.

"Say something, Daddy," Diti pleaded.

"As you know, have I ever lied to you, either directly or indirectly?" Bhushan asked.

"No, but why now?" she asked, sitting up straight and looking him in the eye.

"First of all, neither I nor your mother said anything inappropriate in front of them. His status or religion wouldn't have been an obstacle. The parent must thoroughly check and ensure that your choice is reasonable, right?" Bhushan explained.

"Yes, that's natural. But why are Varghese and his mother suddenly distancing themselves from me?"

"You're asking the same question again. If the reason isn't with us, it must be with them, right?" Bhushan replied.

"Promise?"

"Promise," Bhushan said, patting her back.

"Sorry for doubting you, Daddy," Diti said, getting up and went to her room.

However, she was tormented by the thought that the change in their behaviour must be due to something that happened during the meeting with her parents. She decided to talk to Jessica again.

Meanwhile, Bhushan and Bharti were distressed by her pain. They were worried about how to console her. Bhushan decided to discuss this with his brother Nijaguna. Bharati resigned herself to time, saying, "Kalaya Tasmai Namah" (Time shall cure everything).

*** ___ ***

"Auntie, it's Diti," she said when Jessica opened the door and let her in. Diti had taken leave and arrived at Varghese's house around eleven in the morning. As usual, Varghese had left for the office at 9:30 AM.

"What would you like, coffee or tea?" Jessica asked.

"Nothing, Auntie. I had breakfast and coffee before coming," Diti replied. Jessica seated her on the sofa and sat down in the chair opposite her.

"You didn't go to the office today?" Jessica asked.

"No, Auntie. I took leave to talk to you,"

"What is it?"

"Varghese is not the same with me anymore. Yesterday, he told me bluntly that we shouldn't see or talk to each other anymore.
I came to talk to you about that. Why, Auntie?"
Diti's voice wavered slightly as she sought answers.

Hearing this, Jessica felt relieved. Although she knew her son would obey her, she had a doubt whether his deep love for Diti might make him waver.

'From now on, you should never be with Diti. You can't marry her. Forget about it,' Jessica had sternly told her son the day after Bhushan and Bharti had visited.

"Why, Mom? Why are you telling me this suddenly?" Varghese had asked, his confusion evident.

"Don't ask why, just trust me. I'm saying this for your good," she had replied, her voice firm.

"Fine, for my good, but shouldn't I know what this 'good' is and why? You've always said the same thing when I asked about Dad. I'm not a child anymore. I have the maturity to understand and respond to what you say. Tell me why. I swear on Jesus, I'll never go against your word, but tell me why" Varghese had said, holding her hand, his eyes pleading for an explanation.

"Not now, perhaps some other time" she had assured.

"Alright, listen carefully," and then shared the story of her past life.

*** --- ***

Jessica's original name was Kumari. She belonged to a poor family in a village near Bellary. After passing her SSLC exam, she couldn't continue her education due to poverty and joined Prabathi Printing Press in Bellary as an assistant. An orphan, she was raised by her grandmother. After her grandmother passed away, she secretly married Bhadrappa, who worked with her at the press, in a temple. But three months after their marriage, Bhadrappa died in a railway accident. The same month he passed away, she missed her period for fifteen days. Two weeks later, when she got tested at the hospital, she found out she was pregnant. In desperation, she attempted suicide, but Father from St. Mark's Convent in Bellary saved her and offered her refuge. Jessica (Kumari) told Diti all these events and revealed that Bhadrappa, Bhushan, and Nijaguna were brothers.

"Therefore, Varghese is your paternal uncle's son and hence, your brother. You two cannot marry. Forget about him. And promise me you won't tell anyone, especially Varghese, about this," Jessica said.

Hearing this, Diti felt as if the ground beneath her feet had collapsed, and she was left shaken. The revelation hit her hard, and she struggled to process the implications of what Jessica had just shared. Her mind whirled with thoughts and emotions, leaving her speechless and overwhelmed.

*** ___ ***

"Are you in love with someone?" Javaregowda asked his daughter. They were sitting in her house in Mysore. Apart from them, there was no one else there. After she rejected the IAS suitor, this suspicion arose in him.

"If I am in love...?" Kalavati asked.

"If you had told me earlier, I wouldn't have invited them. You are my only daughter. Why would I stand in the way of your happiness?

Tell me, who is the boy?"

"If I tell you, will you arrange my marriage with him?"

"Of course, tell me who it is," "Would you agree if he belongs to a different caste?" Kalavati inquired, testing the waters.

"Why, what caste is he?"
Javaregowda asked, his curiosity piqued.

"He is not from our caste,"

"Who is it? Tell me directly," he insisted, growing impatient.

"You know him."

"Good, if it's someone I know, even better. Who is it?"

"Dr. Prasad," Kalavati said.

Javaregowda had no inkling that the Prasad she was referring to was the son of Arasayya, who worked in their estate. He couldn't even imagine that possibility.

"If he is a doctor, he must be suitable. Alright, which town is he from, and what do his parents do?" he enquired.

Realising that he didn't understand, Prasad she mentioned, was Arasayya's son, Kalavati hesitated to clarify.

"Why are you hesitating? Don't be afraid, tell me who he is and where he is from. I promise I will arrange your marriage with him grandly," Javaregowda assured her, holding her hand.

"Prasad, the son of Arasayya, who manages our land," she said hesitantly.

Javaregowda's face darkened, and he collapsed back onto the sofa, clutching his chest.

"One minute, I'll make some coffee," Kalavati got up and entered the kitchen.

At that moment, Javaregowda became so angry that he felt like killing her. But he restrained himself, realising he couldn't lose his only daughter. He decided to handle this delicately, knowing that acting out of anger would lead to disaster. He regretted that he had spent money to educate a boy who was now deemed worthy of marrying his daughter. Having been seasoned in politics and strategies, he decided to find a way to avoid this situation.

"Does Prasad know about this?" he asked, sipping his coffee.

"He knows," she replied shortly.

"Alright, come to Hunsur this Saturday. Let's find out your mother's opinion and decide," he said, standing up.

Kalavati, feeling very happy, bowed and touched his feet in reverence.

*** --- ***

"As long as you don't change your decision, this room will be your world," Javaregowda sternly told, locking his daughter Kalavati in a bedroom at Hunsur house, locking the door from the outside.

Kalavati had arrived at their Hunsur home at three o'clock on Saturday afternoon, as her father had instructed when he visited her.

"If I had known you would bring such disgrace upon us, I would have killed you at birth," her mother, Jayamma, had lashed out at her.

Kalavati knew it would be difficult for her parents to accept this marriage, but their cruelty shocked her.

Javaregowda would open the door at mealtimes to bring her food and then lock it again from the outside. Kalavati refused to eat anything except taking water.

Unaware of any of this, Prasad met Javaregowda one morning in his Hunsur MLA office and informed him that he had secured a seat for MS at Mysore Medical College.

"That's great news! Do you need to pay the admission fee?" Javaregowda asked, his tone surprisingly amiable given his usual stern demeanour.

"Yes, sir,"

"How much will it be?"

"Around two lakhs, sir. Once I receive the merit scholarship, the money we pay now will be refunded."

"When is the last date to pay the fee?"

"It should be within months. I'll inform you once it's announced, sir," Prasad said.

"Alright, remind me two days before, and I'll give you the money," he looked at Prasad intently and asked, "Why don't you go abroad to study?"

"I could, sir. I have an offer from a college hospital at the American Medical University. I could work there while pursuing my PG,"

Prasad replied, his voice steady.

"Why did you turn down such a good opportunity?" "My parents didn't want me to go, sir," Prasad said.

After a moment of contemplation, Javaregowda said,
"Good. Come and see me again."

Their meetings were always brief.

*** --- ***

Eight days passed, but Kalavati was not released from the room. As the room had an attached bathroom, she could attend to her daily needs and bathe. Jayamma regularly provided her with necessary clothes and food, but always in Javaregowda's presence. He had not given his wife the room key.

"She has only been drinking water for eight days. I'm worried.

Should we go inside and check on her?" Jayamma cried one morning while preparing to take food to Kalavati.

Javaregowda had not allowed anyone to enter the room. He opened the door completely, and they both went inside. What they saw horrified them.

Kalavati lay emaciated on the bed, unconscious. Her eyes were sunken, and her cheeks were wrinkled. She could barely open her eyes and had no strength to speak. Jayamma, holding her daughter, cried,

"Oh, my poor child!"

"Give her water and sugar water immediately," Javaregowda instructed, and then went downstairs to call his trusted assistant, urgently requesting an ambulance to take them to Mysore.

An ambulance arrived at the house, and with the help of nurses, they placed Kalavati inside and drove to a private hospital in

Mysore. Javaregowda and Jayamma followed in their car.

Kalavati had been pouring all the food given to her into the toilet and washing the plates to hide the fact that she wasn't eating.

After admitting Kalavati to a deluxe family special room and examining her, the doctor, after hearing the details from Javaregowda, immediately started her on a glucose drip, monitored her flow, and advised the duty nurse accordingly. The doctor assured them, "There's no need to worry. She will recover once she receives a few bottles of glucose."

Hearing the news, Prasad arrived at the hospital.

He was unaware of what had happened.

"What happened, sir? What did the doctor say? I'll go and ask them," he said, walking towards the doctor's room.

"Don't meet them; I'll tell you everything. Come with me," Javaregowda said.

He got him seated in his car and drove towards the Lalitha Mahal Palace. Before leaving, he told his wife,

"We'll be back in an hour. Stay with her. If there's anything urgent call me."

At a secluded spot near the foothills of Chamundi Hill, close to the palace Lalitha Mahal, he parked the car, opened the windows, and made Prasad, who was sitting in the back seat, sit beside him. Prasad, anxious and uncomfortable, tried to sit as far from Javaregowda as possible.

"Have I ever caused you any trouble?"
Javaregowda asked, staring at Prasad.

Perplexed by the question, Prasad said, "What are you saying, sir? It's only because of your kindness that I'm a doctor today. I can never repay your debt, not even in seven lifetimes."

"That's your humility, Prasad. I'm glad. If you get an opportunity to repay this debt in this lifetime, will you do it?" he asked, his gaze intense.

"Sir. Without any doubt, tell me. No matter how difficult it is, I'll do it for you, even if it costs my life," Prasad said, his eyes filling with tears.

During his school days, when other boys and teachers distanced themselves and looked down on him, Javaregowda had financially supported him throughout, making him a doctor. Prasad had immense reverence for him. However, in matters of Kalavati, he saw her more as a childhood companion rather than Javaregowda's daughter, a pure love encouraged by her. It never felt wrong to him.

"I'll get straight to the point. Kala wants to marry you. This has come as a shocking blow to us. As you know, it is impossible. An IAS officer, of our caste, whose father is also an MLA like me, came to our house with his parents to see her. If she agrees, I'll arrange a grand wedding for her, at Lalitha Mahal Palace, in the presence of the Chief Minister and dignitaries. amid this expectation and joy, Kala's desire is like a bolt of lightning. Now, I need your help," he said.

Prasad, who genuinely believed that his gratitude towards Javaregowda, who had guided him like a God, was far more important than Kalavati's love, requested, "Tell me, sir, what should I do?"

"You mentioned that you have a job offer from a hospital in America. Is that still available?"

"Yes, sir." "Alright, take that job and go to America. I'll cover all the expenses. Work there and pursue your PG. If Kala asks, firmly reject her. Think of her as your sister and protect my honour," Javaregowda said, holding his hand, his voice choked with emotion.

"Sir. I swear on Mother Chamundeshwari, I'll stay away from Kala," adding emotionally, "If I may, I have one request, sir."

"What is it?"

"I'll do my PG here, in Gulbarga, far away from Kalavati. Please don't worry about it, sir. Please agree to this."

"What's stopping you from going to America?"

"I'm scared to leave my ageing parents, and go so far away sir," he pleaded "Don't be afraid of that. Your parents have always been under my care since you were born. They have diligently managed our land and gardens. When Indira Gandhi implemented the Land Reforms Act, declaring 'Land belongs to those who till it,' your father refused to declare ownership despite all the persuasion from the Dalit Sangharsha Samiti leaders of your village, Ratnapuri Colony. That has always stayed in my mind. I regard your father as my brother. If you stay here, Kalavati will bring trouble to both of us. I'll talk to your parents and convince them. Establish contact with the American hospital via letters or computer communication and take the job. Go to Bangalore one day and get your passport made. In America, you will receive respect and happiness that you won't find here. Go, it will be good for you. You will find a new identity and life there. Your future will be much brighter than it would be here," Javaregowda assured, his tone persuasive.

Prasad, deeply moved and conflicted, nodded in agreement.

"I'll do as you say, sir. I'll take the job in America and ensure that Kala's future remains undisturbed. Thank you for your guidance and support," he was weeping.

"Good, Prasad. You are doing the right thing. This will secure, not only your future but also the harmony and honour of my family,"

*** --- ***

Diti returned home from Jessica's house. As Bhushan had gone to college, only Bharati was at home.

"Is this true, Mom?" she asked.

"What is?" Bharti replied.

"I went to Jessica's Auntie's house,"

"Really? Why now?"

"When I met Varghese at the office yesterday, he said, 'Our marriage is impossible. So let's stay away from each other.' When I asked why, he said his mother didn't approve and that he didn't want to hurt her. So both of us should stay apart. When I asked why she said that, he said he didn't know. That's why I went to ask her."

"What did she say?"

"I can't believe what she told me," Bharti remained silent.

"She says Varghese's father is Dad's elder brother. Is that believable?" Diti asked.

Bharti remained silent again.

"Did she tell you the same thing?"

"When we came home, Bhushan informed me about it as I was not there when they discussed it. " Bharati said.

"I don't believe it,"

"Why not?"

"I think you're making up things to stop our marriage."

"Look, Diti, we have no reason to break your friendship or relationship. Don't make assumptions. Your dad learned this from Jessica, and it was entirely co-incidental. Neither she nor your dad fabricated anything. To confirm this, your dad plans to visit Jessica's house this Sunday with your Nijaguna uncle. You should go with them,"

"Will you come too?" Feeling somewhat reassured by her mother's words, Diti asked "First, talk to your dad this evening when he returns from college. Once the visit is confirmed, we'll decide who will go," Bharti said.

*** ___ ***

That evening, while having coffee after Bhushan returned from college, Diti said, "Daddy, I wanted to ask you something."

"What is it, dear?"

"Varghese's mother says his father is like your elder brother. Is that true?"

"Yes, it seems so. I didn't know Varghese was my brother's son. It was his mother, Jessica who told me this,"

"How, Daddy? Explain clearly, what happened?"

Bhushan remained silent for a moment, sipping his coffee. After finishing his last sip, he said, "Varghese mentioned that his father worked in a printing press in Bellary years ago when he visited our house in Birmingham. When we visited her on that day, I mentioned that my brother also worked in the same press.

When I told Jessica this, she asked for his name. As soon as I mentioned his name, her face darkened, and she said, 'This relationship can't happen.' When I asked why, she didn't give any details and ended the conversation abruptly by saying, 'My son and your daughter are siblings.' As this was shocking news for her, I didn't probe further."

"Are you sure the person who worked in that press was your brother? Mom told me, you were in Thanjavur and only came to Bangalore after Anuradha Auntie's marriage, right? Did you ever visit Bellary to meet him?" Diti asked.

"That's true. I've never been to Bellary to see him. He passed away in a railway accident before I came to Bangalore from Thanjavur. This is what I heard from your uncle Nijaguna. He, along with your other uncle Kotrappa, went there, brought back his body, and performed the last rites in our hometown, Kottur. That is what I heard from my brother Nijaguna," he paused and said, "Can you do me a favour?"

"What, Daddy?"

"Can you visit Jessica's house again and ask if we can come over one Sunday morning?"

"Who do you mean by 'we'?"

"Me, you, and your uncle," "Does Guni uncle know about this?"

"Yes, I informed him after returning from Jessica's house. He also wants to meet her."

"Have you told him about our relationship?"

"No."

"Then why should we go with him?"

Bhushan laughed and said, "My dear, this is no more, just about you and Varghese now. It's about our brother Bhadrappa and his son's question. Do you remember our lineage?"

"Of course, Daddy, we are from the Veerashaiva Veerashetty lineage, right?"

"Correct. Do you know that John Varghese also belongs to the Veerashetti lineage?"

Diti's face darkened, and without saying anything, she left for her room.

*** ___ ***

Determined to get to the bottom of the matter, Diti went to the office the next day. In the evening, she went to Varghese's house and spoke with Jessica.

Varghese was in his room while she was talking to her.

"Does Varghese know about this, Auntie?" she asked after being briefed.

"No, dear. I only found out while talking to your dad," Jessica replied.

"Why not ?"

"Why should he know all this? It's enough if you stop coming to our house and end your friendship with him. I've suffered enough in my life. Now that my son has started working and we're living in some peace, please leave us to ourselves," Jessica pleaded with folded hands.

"I can't leave it at that, Auntie."

"Why not?"

"Daddy says he and my uncle Nijaguna want to meet you. He asked if they could come this Sunday,"

"Why do they want to meet?"

"They want to know about Varghese's father, Auntie."

"What do they need to know? It's all a forgotten story. There's nothing to tell or ask. They don't need to meet me. Please tell them that. And you should stop coming to our house. Please leave us alone," Jessica said just as Varghese emerged and overheard his mother.

"What's the matter, Mom?" he asked.

"Well, it's..." Diti began "I'll tell Varghese later. It's getting late for you; you should head home before it gets dark," Jessica interrupted.

Diti, feeling dejected, picked up her bag and left.
Varghese walked her to her car and then went back upstairs.

"What's the matter, Mom?" he asked again, sensing the tension.

"Drink your coffee first," Jessica said, placing a cup of coffee in front of him.

"Listen, John, I'm going to tell you something, and you need to listen and follow what I say. Don't ask why. I'm saying this for both our sakes, alright?" she said.

"Alright, Mom, tell me," "Diti is your sister, so you can't marry her. You need to stay away from her and keep her away too. If possible, find a job in a faraway place like Gulbarga or some city in North India. We'll live peacefully there. We don't need this Bangalore," she said, her voice firm.

"What are you saying, Mom? How can Diti be my sister?" Varghese asked, bewildered.

"Your father and Diti's father are brothers. Don't ask anything more," Jessica said, heading into the kitchen.

Varghese felt shattered and collapsed into his seat, his mind reeling from the revelation.

*** ___ ***

When Dithi returned home, Bhushan and Bharati were seated on the sofa watching TV. Dithi collapsed onto the sofa, tossing her laptop bag aside.

"Was the workload heavy at the office?" Bhushan asked, seeing his daughter throw her laptop bag and stretch out her legs.

"I went to Varghese's house," she said in a defeated voice!

"Did you tell them we plan to visit on Sunday?"

"I did."

"What did she say?"

"She said no one should go there and requested to leave them alone," Diti burst into tears. she was crying.

Bharati, who had just brought a cup of coffee, placed it on the table and sat beside her, hugging her. Dithi buried her face in her mother's lap and sobbed. Bhushan moved closer and patted her back.

"Why is this happening to me? What crime have I committed to deserve this punishment?"

"This is fate's play, dear. It's not your fault. Have you heard the story of Oedipus?" Bhushan asked.

Dithi remained silent.

"It's relevant to this situation, so. listen. Even if you know it, listen again," Bhushan said.

"Oedipus was a king in Greek mythology. When he was born, a prophecy said he would kill his father and marry his mother. So his father ordered his servants to take the baby to the forest and kill him. But the servants couldn't bring themselves to kill it and left the baby..."

"Stop, Daddy. I've read it. It's just a myth, not a real event.
But what's happening to me is real," she said, got up, and rushed towards her room.

"What should we do now, Bhushan?"

"I don't know. For now, let's not force her to talk. Let's leave her alone. Let us hope that time will provide a solution. I'll go to my brother's house tomorrow evening after college to discuss this with him. Let's see what he suggests," Bhushan said.

*** ___ ***

"Why have you suddenly appeared?" Aditi asked when Prasad unexpectedly came to her house that evening.

"I wanted to talk to you," Prasad replied.

"Let's have some coffee first," Aditi suggested.

"Let's sit in the Coffee Day near the park and talk over coffee,"

Prasad said, standing up.

"Wait a minute, I'll be right back," Aditi said, going to her room.

She came down after a few minutes, having changed her clothes and carrying her purse. They walked towards Coffee Day.

"I'm not joining PG here," Prasad said as they sat at a table in the corner of the Coffee Day Restaurant next to Bhashyam Park.

"Why? What happened?" Aditi asked anxiously.

"I got a job at a hospital in Chicago, USA.
I'm going to America.
I've come to get my passport and visa."

"Why did you make this decision suddenly? In our last meeting, you talked about joining PG in Mysore and marrying your childhood friend?"

Aditi was startled at the breaking news.

"That's all in the past now"

"What do you mean?"

Prasad remained silent, staring at the wall and sipping his coffee.

Aditi sensed that something serious must have happened.

"Have you heard the saying, 'Man proposes, God disposes'?"

"Isn't that the cliché'?" she laughed, "What happened? Tell me," "I thought I would do my PG, but that's not happening. I thought I would marry Kala, but that's not happening either. This isn't a cliché, nor is it fate. It's not divine intervention; it's human cruelty," Prasad said.

Aditi, moved by his words and the pain behind them, remained silent, staring.

"Sorry, am I rambling?" he gave a dry smile.

Aditi remained silent, not reacting.

"This is what happened," Prasad continued, explaining in detail how Kalavati was hospitalised and his conversation with Javaregowda.

Aditi listened with a mixed expression.
"Why did you agree to leave for USA?"

"What else could I do?"

"Why didn't you stand your ground and say no?"

"It's not as easy as it sounds."

"Why? What makes it difficult?"

"You won't understand, sorry," Prasad said.

"What do you mean?"

"How can I defy the people who raised me to this point? It's impossible."

"What will you tell that girl ?"

" I will tell her, 'I thought I loved you, but in reality, I was in love with my medical college classmate, Aditi. I'm sorry, forget me." He looked at her.

"Isn't that dangerous?"

"How?"

"What if she harms herself again? Who will be responsible for that?"

"But I won't tell her that now."

"Then when will you tell her?"

"After I go to America. I'll write her a letter from there."

"Isn't it wrong to lie to her?"

"What lie?"

"I feel you're telling her not one but two lies."

"How?"

"First, that you don't love her."

"And the second?"

"That you love me. Tell me the truth, do you love me and If I say yesex, will you marry me?"

Prasad was startled by her second question.

"We're good friends as classmates, that's all. It's just friendship. But what I intend to tell her is just an excuse. excuse. That's all, nothing more."

"Don't you think it might hurt me?"

"Sorry, perhaps I was insensitive. Forgive me."

"No, no, not like that. I love you, and if you accept me, I am ready to marry you?"

Prasad was surprised.

"Sorry, I never saw you in that light,"

"How do you feel now that I have confessed it?"

"Forgive me,
you don't understand what you're saying and its consequences."

"So, you think I'm immature?"

"Sorry, you're naive and unaware of the ways of this society. Please don't be upset with my words, if they sound harsh."

"What do you mean?"

"Look, in this country, what is called Hinduism, is in fact, against humanity.

As I understand, it's not a religion at all. It's a conspiracy by some selfish people."

"Why do you think so?"

"It's not just my opinion; it's a fact. The so-called Sanatana Hindus say there are four varnas: Brahmin, Kshatriya, Vaishya, and Shudra. I don't belong to any of these four classes. They call me Panchama, the fifth one, untouchable and unworthy of being touched. Yet, they still call me a Hindu. It's a huge irony," he laughed. "But the Hindu society rejects me as untouchable. These Hindus, who keep cows, dogs, and cats inside their homes, won't even let me near their doorstep. Even if I walk down the street where these so-called high-caste people live, they consider the street polluted. We are not allowed inside Hindu temples or Restaurants. Outside the Restaurants, we have separate plates and cups for us. We have to wash them ourselves and keep them there. If another untouchable comes, they have to use those. Yes, they believe I'm dirt and treat me that way," Prasad was lost in his thoughts of which he was painfully aware.

"Stop, stop, don't talk nonsense and hurt me. These must be your imagination. Haven't you mingled with everyone, studied, and become a doctor? Aren't we sitting in a nice Restaurant now? Don't tell lies," Aditi said, interrupting him angrily.

Prasad smiled inwardly at her naivety.

"What you see is true for a city like Bangalore. This environment and behaviour exist only in cities where money is the only thing that matters. About eighty per cent of Hindus live in villages, and nothing happens there without caste considerations."

"Does our law accept this untouchability you're talking about?"

"True, the law doesn't accept it. But the law is not able to stop this and it never will be," Prasad said with a sardonic smile.

"If it's not legal, why can't it be stopped?"

"Let me tell you about a recent incident. Mahadev, a friend of mine and two years senior to me in medical college is a government doctor. He's from a village in Gulbarga district. There's a big lake in that village that everyone uses. People wash clothes, bathe, and give water to their cattle there. But so-called untouchables are not allowed to touch the lake's water.

Once, when Dr Mahadev went to his village, he gathered the Dalits and tried to use the lake's water with police protection. The prominent Lingayats of the village met him and said, 'According to the law, you can use the lake's water. If we obstruct you, we'll be jailed. So we won't obstruct you. But know this, once you touch the lake's water, the entire village will stop using it. We've decided this in a meeting of all community leaders.' After hearing this, Dr. Mahadev was shocked and stopped the movement, returning to the city. I asked him why he stopped the movement. He said, 'In our village of six thousand people, there are about six hundred Dalits. If

I continued the movement and the Dalits touched the lake's water, the lake would have become just a Dalit lake. They said they would boycott the lake we touched. What can the law do here? If we touched the lake's water, thousands of people in our village would have been troubled. So I came back, deciding to let it be.' See how it is? Can the law force other castes to use the lake's water with Dalits? What needs to change is the mindset of these other castes. That won't happen in our villages.

See, I explained all this because, when Hindus treat us this way, how can I marry Kala or you and lead a peaceful life? It's clear to me that it's impossible. So, forgive me, I've decided to go to America, convert to Christianity, marry someone I like there, and lead a peaceful life. You said you love me. I'll always cherish your confession. It's getting late; let's go,"

*** --- ***

One morning, Jessica suddenly complained of chest pain. That day, Varghese took leave from his office and rushed her to the nearby Jayadeva Hospital. After examining her, the doctor said she needed to stay in the hospital for four days to undergo an ECG, angiography, and other tests. Following the doctor's advice, Varghese admitted her to the hospital and took a week's leave from the office. Hearing about this, Diti also came to the hospital to talk to and reassure her.

The next day, the doctor said, "Ninety per cent of the blood vessels in her heart are blocked, and she urgently needs bypass surgery," Varghese was devastated. Diti comforted him and informed her parents about the situation.

That evening, Bhushan, Bharati, Nijaguna, and Aditi visited the hospital to see her.

"You came to the printing press where I worked many years ago. My employer, Shantarudrappa, asked me to bring you a cup of tea. I now remember you," Jessica said addressing Nijaguna.

Following her request, only two of them were present in the special ward.

"Yes, when I came looking for my brother Bhadrappa, a woman there had brought me tea that day; I know now that it was you," Nijaguna said, "How did you recognise that?"

"I listened carefully to everything you said to him that day. Because my husband, your brother, and I were already married by then," Jessica admitted.

"Then you could have met me outside and discussed," Nijaguna said.

"How could I tell you? We hadn't married formally in front of witnesses. We exchanged garlands and became husband and wife in a temple, with only a co-worker from our press as a witness. We hadn't even told Shantarudrappa about it. It was a secret between the three of us," she explained.

"The day your brother died in the accident, I attempted suicide by jumping into a canal outside the city. Father Joshua, who was there, jumped into the canal and saved me. When he found out I was an orphan and pregnant, he admitted me to the hospital. From that moment, I became a new person. Your brother had a drinking habit, it's true. But otherwise, he was a very good man. When I expressed my desire to marry him, he refused, saying, 'Why would you marry someone like me? Don't.' I forced him into marriage. But the accident took him away. But he didn't leave me alone," Jessica recounted sadly.

"Varghese gave meaning to my life. Now, seeing him reunited with his family makes me very happy. Tomorrow, I have bypass surgery. I don't know if I'll come out of it healthy or die on the operating table. If I die, please take care Varghese..." She folded her hands.

"Please don't talk like that. Nothing will happen to you. You'll come home safe after the operation," Nijaguna interrupted, trying to reassure her.

*** ___ ***

Jessica underwent bypass surgery, but unfortunately, she died on the operating table due to excessive bleeding. Nijaguna suggested performing her last rites at the Veerashaiva Rudrabhoomi in Chamarajpet, Bangalore. Varghese didn't agree and took her body to the church in Bellary, where Father Joshua conducted the funeral rites at the Christian cemetery. Nijaguna and Bhushan accompanied him. Although Diti wanted to go, Varghese and the others disagreed, hence she didn't go.

Epilogue

- Three months have passed since all these events. During this period, Varadaraja Iyengar from Thanjavur passed away due to old age. Before his death, Aditi agreed to marry Jayakeerthi, fulfilling his final wish. She had promised her grandfather that she would set up a nursing home in Thanjavur after graduation.

- "My daughter didn't fulfill my wish, but my granddaughter will," Varadaraja Iyengar said before passing away, peacefully.

- Dr. Prasad is now settled in the USA as a doctor in a hospital in Chicago. Kalavati tried every possible way to contact him but failed. Now she immersed herself in her court work, trying to be pragmatic and forget the past events as a distant dream. Javaregowda and his wife found solace in the relief that she didn't marry a Dalit boy.

- John Varghese and Diti are now working and settled in London.

- Before flying to London, Diti confided the news only in Aditi.

*** ___ ***

"Why did you fly so suddenly without informing us, Diti?" Bharati asked her over the phone.

" Mom, my name is now Elizabeth Varghese, and I'm three months along"

Diti replied before hanging up the phone.